ALTERRA

ALTERRA

Matthew Buscemi

Published by Matthew Buscemi, 2020
Seattle, Washington USA

ISBN 978-1-62802-023-6

Copyright © Matthew Buscemi 2016
Cover Illustration Copyright © Zhivko Zhelev 2020

Typeset by Matthew Buscemi in Mantonico with Gotham display

To Scott
for the trampoline

TABLE OF CONTENTS

PROLOGUE

Book of Salvation, Chapter 1, Verses 6-20

⁶ And then did the Divine One make a race of humans upon Asura. He smiled upon his final creation, and like each of his creations before, the humans could not comprehend him. They did not smile back. They ran off into the forests, amongst the boars and rabbits and deer and squirrels.

⁷ The Divine One, loving his creations deeply, decided that, to just this last one, the humans, he would give the capacity to understand his true form.

⁸ The Divine Fire coursed through the veins of the humans of Asura, and they did awaken.

[9] They looked up at their creator, and they comprehended him, and they smiled.

[10] Winter came and many of the humans grew cold. Many died of hunger and disease. With their newfound comprehension, they looked upon the Divine One pleadingly. Being ever merciful, the Divine One gave them the knowledge of fire, the knowledge of hunting, and the handicraft skills to make clothing out of fur pelts.

[11] Many happy years passed. The humans hunted game in the forests and drank fresh water from the rivers. But one year, the rain was sparse. Few fruits grew upon the trees, and game became scarce. The humans were forced to march many miles to find greener pastures, and once again, many died.

[12] The Divine One at first resisted the temptation to give them more. He had given them too much of his knowledge already. Parents wept as they buried dead children. The humans looked up at him with scorn in their eyes and ire in their

hearts. Would he not help them again? Did he hate them, after all? No, the Divine One decided. He did not.

[13] Against his better judgment, the Divine One gave the humans the knowledge of agriculture and irrigation. He added hoes and scythes to their arsenal of bows and spears. The humans were able to settle and to stockpile food. In years of drought, they dipped into their reserves.

[14] One year, the humans built a temple to the Divine One, that they might pray to and worship him. When they sat in their temple, deep in their adoration, he could interpret their thoughts and feelings, loose collections of images and emotions. Their desire was so clear in its purpose and powerful in its measure, that it brought the Divine One to the brink of despair.

[15] "No," the Divine One said. "No, I will not grant you all my powers. After many trials and many errors, after much suffering and regret, I have come to be, I hope, a good and decent God.

[16] "Were I to give you everything, all of my ability to perceive, all of my ability to comprehend, you too would have many trials and many errors. You too would have to learn to be good and decent. Many of you would turn toward your darker nature, and the end of your collective path, either enlightenment or devastation, would be uncertain. I will not do it."

[17] The humans of Asura persisted in visiting their temple. Their numbers swelled. More settlements were founded and more temples built. The humans pleaded with their thoughts and feelings. They yearned to know–to understand.

[18] The Divine One, a cacophony of conflicting emotions, eventually relented. "All right," he said. "I will give you the last of my abilities. With this, you will be my equal but for my wisdom and millennia of experiences. Be good to each other. Be kind. And grow wise, or this power will undo you and the entire world you inhabit."

[19] And then the Divine One bestowed the last of his powers upon the humans of Asura.

[20] He gave them words.

AESTHETIC

[Le]

"Initiate Le." The voice pierced my trance. "Initiate Le!"

"Sorry, sir."

Master Kierk crossed his arms and raised his eyebrows. The irate eyes of my classmates fell upon me. I tried to ignore them, to find my place on the holographic projection of the Writ atop my desk, but—

"Verse twenty-one." Master Kierk sighed and made a rolling motion with his hand.

My eyes caught Shey's, and his gaze bore into me with the strength of a sand weevil's sixteen feet.

I managed to find the holographic numeral twenty-one, and I gulped.

"The men and women of Asura found names for all the things, living and unliving, within their world. They named all the lights and shapes in the sky, and all the tools they had learned to create."

The girl behind me began verse twenty-two, her voice prim and proper. I exhaled as silently as I could and leaned back.

Shey gazed at me still from two aisles over. Irritation welled up in my stomach. I narrowed my eyes at him, and he turned away.

A message appeared alongside the Writ, projected from my handy. "I'll bet you forgot about tonight, too."

I hadn't forgotten, though I'd wanted to.

Urges for... something flickered within my brain. I could leave him, take control of my life. Things had been so simple two years ago. Now we had to choose. And Shey—University, University, University. It had been months since we'd discussed anything else.

I wasn't feeling it. Every so often, I'd find my gaze straying up the hill toward the Monastery, when Shey wasn't around, of course, and—

The guy sitting one desk over spoke. "The technologs said, 'Your ways are sick. You are a menace.' The avatars said, 'Our ways are our own. We will not threaten you. We wish to live as we are.' The technologs were more powerful, and they cast the avatars out, to another world entirely. The avatars wept for losing their Divine One, just as they named their new world. They called it Alterra."

And then the guy, the one who had just recited the verse, glanced my way ever so slightly. His lip turned up into a grin—just a bit. I'd seen him around. He didn't talk to others much. What was his name again?

The moment passed and he hunched over his desk, cradling his head in his arms and gazing into his projection of the Writ.

I wondered what options had been lost for my relationship with Shey. I realized that I resented him and his stupid Resurgence meetings. Such a waste of time.

I put my head on my desk, too and gazed into the Writ, but found neither solace nor answers within its words.

Shey strode down the path beside me, our sandals crunching over the loose sand.

The stars peeked out from just behind the mountains. I raised my head and looked at the hundreds of bright lights and the bluish froth splayed through them, running north to south. The Writ told that the sky of Asura had not looked like this. That world's galaxy had a different shape to its spiral arm. I wondered if that were true.

"You hungry?" Shey asked.

"No." I realized I'd let annoyance slip into my voice, and that wasn't fair to Shey, but I really wasn't.

Shey made a show of sighing deeply. "Maybe we could do our math homework together after the meeting?"

I mumbled something that was probably incoherent.

A part of me liked that Shey was trying. That was how we'd met, after all. I'd found him in the Bibliotech, his tussled brown hair draped over a projection of equations and lines and graphs. He'd looked up at me and smiled. We'd recognized each other from class and done our homework together.

"Yeah, sure." I tried to sound eager, or maybe just kind.

I felt like I failed.

We passed the wall of metal slabs with yellow and black stripes of tape plastered over them. This was the edge of Zone H, the one running the length of the river from the arboretum down to the still grass meadows.

A spark of miniature lightning burst up over the walls, crackling above our heads.

Shey looked at it with disdain.

"We could fix this," he gestured. "If we were allowed."

"C'mon, Shey." I didn't bother hiding my irritation.

"Barbaric," he muttered.

We trudged onward in silence.

Before long, the wall gave way, drifting out into the sands and then the river. Still grass appeared beside the path, growing taller as we approached the arboretum. It was tall this time of year, some blades nearly as tall as me. They hung in the air, their curves like sickles, unbending and unmoving, even in the wind. Their tips drifted upward, terminating in rounded stubs.

Had the still grass been sharp, it would be deadly.

Shey opened the glass doors to the arboretum. We both waited, awkwardly. He gestured with his hand. I entered, and he followed.

Most of the other Resurgents were milling about already. A tank served up beverages in the corner next to a tray of tiny sandwiches and cakes. I truly wasn't hungry, but the hospitality table was the easiest way to avoid having to talk to anyone at these things, I had learned. I abandoned Shey at the door, ran to the tank, poured myself a cup of soda and grabbed a sandwich off the table.

The arboretum we stood in was a two-level structure of glass walls and partitions. The second story had a glass floor, making every room visible from every location within it. Kinda eery, but at least consistent with the Resurgence.

I did like the air in here though. It always smelled fresh. As long as I could avoid conversation, it would stay that way.

I drifted away from Shey, over to a holographic poster that sputtered over the glass wall. It depicted meager scientists huddled over broken lab equipment. Monks stood on a sandy hill above them, wielding swords and spears laced with monktech wires and light nodes.

"OPPRESSION," the poster declared in bold type.

I looked back over the crowd of Resurgents. They wore the nicest clothes of all the people in Rig. They talked jovially and openly with one another. They acted like Shey.

'Oppressed' was honestly the last descriptor that came to mind.

"Hello."

I turned from the poster, just as the image shifted. A girl stood beside me, probably just a few years older than me. She held a drink. Her eyes betrayed her interest.

"Hi," I stammered.

"I'm Fera."

"Le."

"Is this your first time here?"

This happened too often. I did my best not to seem too uncomfortable. "No. I'm here with my boyfriend."

The spark in her eyes dissipated. She smiled bemusedly. For a moment, her expression betrayed her anxiety and self-reproach. She covered them quickly. "And he is?"

"Shey." I nodded across the room. He had taken a spot at a table behind a pair of hanging plants with long, green leaves. A man and woman in their thirties or forties, probably a couple, sat with him. From their body language, Shey had already begun his typical rant about the glory of the sciences and vulgarity of 'plebian believers.'

Fera smiled warmly. "He looks very passionate."

My chortle caught in my throat and I coughed instead.

"You all right?" Fera put her hand on my back.

"I'm fine," I wheezed between fits.

Fera set down her glass. "You need some air. Come on."

She grabbed my hand and pulled me outdoors.

The chatter of the Resurgence fell away into quiet night as we exited, and I took deep breaths until the coughing subsided. "Thanks," I said.

"I don't like these Resurgence meetings, either, honestly," Fera said.

I shot her a glance. "Then why do you come?"

Her gaze met mine coldly.

"Whatever." I shrugged. "Sorry."

Her brow fell a bit, and her smile faded to a frown.

"I'm not judging," I tried. "Honestly, I'm sort of in the same boat. I mean, look at Shey. He's handsome. He's smart. Hell, he's not just smart, he's a fucking genius. I should be on my hands and knees, praising the Divine One for being so kind to me."

Fera nodded. "You don't want to go to University, do you? Would you choose Monastery instead, though?"

I threw up my arms. I almost yelled, but I closed my eyes before I opened my mouth. I lowered my arms slowly and took a deep breath. "I don't know what I want. I just... I hate how he and everyone else, but him especially, they all *assume* that I'm going to choose University. Like choosing Monastery is stupid."

Fera nodded to the bustling crowd enclosed behind the glass. "That's how they think in there."

"Do you honestly believe we should overpower the monks? Give the University control of the portal? They don't say it, but that's what they want."

Fera rolled her eyes and waved her hand. "If my future husband wants to worry about that, I'll let him."

My turn to cross my arms. "And what makes you shy away from University yourself? Can't you just enroll at Monastery?"

A look of pain came over her face, just momentarily. She covered it up. She was good at that.

Fera turned to me. "You can choose? Whichever one, and your parents would be okay?"

I shrugged. "Sure. My parents would be fine. It's just...

Well, I know University would take me. Not so sure about Monastery."

"But you're not sure. If you have the choice, don't spend one minute more doing something you don't want. Choose what's best for you. The longer you stick to a rut, the harder it is to leave."

A wave of something passed over me. My skin tingled. I stood up straighter and smiled. "Let's go then." I began to walk away, down the path through the still grass.

"Go?" Fera ran to catch up with me. "We just got here."

"Honestly, it's just like you said. It's like I've been living someone else's life, and I don't want another minute of it." I was beaming. I hadn't felt this way in... I couldn't remember how long.

Fera chuckled and strode confidently alongside me while wind whistled through the still grass.

"Shey's pretty cute, actually."

"He has his moments."

An awkward silence.

"My parents won't let me enroll in Monastery," Fera said. Her eyes had fallen to the ground.

"Have you tried emancipation?" I turned to her.

She nodded. "Denied."

It all came together in my head. "Married for a year—
"

"—And I'll have full legal control over my own enrollment."

I nodded back toward the distant glow of the arboretum. "I take it mom and dad like those types."

Fera was practically stomping. I spotted wet streaks beneath her eyes.

"Well, you can have Shey if you want."

She smiled and punched me in the shoulder. "Thank you, Le."

We continued on, talking as we went. She led me through a fairly well-to-do part of Rig, around Zone C, to a modest house, two stories tall.

I asked if she wanted to hang out again, and she said that'd be great. We made plans to get lunch next freeday.

I strode away from her house feeling as though a pressure had been lifted from my shoulders. Renewed energy drove me home. I took up into a jog, and the dry wind burst at my face.

The roads were empty. Lights glowed from house windows. Families sat with each other around tables, reading, playing games, or telling stories. I found myself wondering what my parents were doing. I imagined dad on the sofa with a novel and mom at her art table, manipulating gravity with her hands. I couldn't walk twenty meters through this city without spotting one of her sculptures decorating a boardwalk or planter or something.

My parents were good people. Kind people. Unlike Shey's.

I felt lucky for that.

I rounded a bend, and the houses disappeared on my

left, the lights along with them. The long, dark wall of Zone H appeared. Energy still crackled overtop it.

I spotted movement in the distance. Was it—? No. No! Someone was pulling a slab of the Zone H wall away!

I broke into a run, careening down the street toward the shifting, stuttering edge of the demarcation that should not—could not—move.

The wall stuttered back into place just as I approached.

I ran my hands over the edge, feeling the indentation where two segments of the wall met. I stuck my fingers between them and pulled. The wall gave, moving outward just a centimeter.

I lurched backward and stumbled over my own feet. I caught myself on the ground and glared at the narrow breach that seemed a gaping chasm.

The gap lurched open wider. A face appeared from within, and my heart nearly stopped.

I found myself staring. A guy. Red-brown hair. Bright eyes. His skin browner than mine, but not quite black.

I stood up slowly, and he stared at me, our eyes locked.

"You're—" I stammered. "Y-you're in Religion. You sit next to me."

"Are you coming in or not?" he said.

"In? Into a *zone*?"

He smiled sarcastically and nodded. "In two seconds I'm closing the wall again."

I hate danger. Despise it.

But something else struck me, took control of me just

then.

I stood. I walked forward. I passed between the diagonal yellow and black stripes. The guy beside me pulled the wall shut.

An ambient greenish-blue glow illuminated a verdant forest. I recognized all these plants. Probably every one of them was represented in the arboretum. But here they grew dense, wild, and uncontrolled, twisting and weaving in and out of one another.

Green pinpoints of brilliant light flitted about the space. Every so often, two would collide and explode into a crackling burst of electricity. The momentary flares cast shadows through the viney, twisting sea of plants.

The croaks of gemma toads emanated from over the hill. I didn't realize how close this was to the river.

"The nanites..." I muttered.

"You'll be fine," my new friend said. He put his hand on my shoulder and I rushed with excitement. I hadn't felt that sensation since Shey and I had spent our first night together.

I stuffed my hands in my pockets, awash with guilt, and I looked at the ground.

The hand left my shoulder. "Sorry... I didn't mean to make you uncomfortable."

"It's not— You don't—" I struggled, my lips flapping wildly, but silently. I couldn't find words.

"What's your name?" His eyes turned kind again.

"Le. Yours?"

"Stok."

"Nice to meet you."

"It's great to finally talk to you."

"You mean, you—?"

He blushed. "I noticed you the first day of Religion class. I didn't think you noticed me though."

My turn to blush.

"It's okay," he continued. "I mean, I understand. You have a boyfriend, so you wouldn't be—" He didn't seem to know how to finish sentences any better than I did.

"Stok?"

"Yeah?"

"Why aren't our bodies being torn apart by malevolent robots?"

Stok rolled his eyes and pushed into the forest. "They're not malevolent."

I followed after. "Then the Writ is wrong?"

"Yes."

"But the University says the nanites' programming can't be recompiled."

"They're wrong too."

I furrowed my brow. That was a new one to me. Either you sided with the monks of the Monastery, in which case you shunned all technology save monktech and embraced the unfathomable spiritual depths of the universe, or you sided with the professors of the University, in which case you embraced technological development at any cost and turned your nose up at the Writ, calling it stupid and backward.

Defying both? I'd never considered it.

"What's in here, Stok?"

"Beauty." He surged forward.

The green lights seemed drawn to our bodies, drifting toward us in waves. Nanite lumens, I presumed. Some even touched my skin. I flinched at first, but they clung harmlessly before flittering away.

The ground turned upward, and the trees and grasses became sparser. We mounted a rocky embankment overlooking the river. On the other side, the landscape lay dappled with still grass and wanwan trees and ardrok bushes, on and on, upward, growing drier and sparser, until the plants gave way to sandy, mountainous dunes.

The stars peeked out from behind them.

Stok sat down and let his feet hang over the edge. "I've been up and down the river ten kilometers each direction. This is the only significant rise on our side. And it's behind that stupid wall."

I sat down beside him. "If the nanites aren't dangerous, why the walls? Why tell everyone they're lethal?"

"Fear," Stok said sadly. "Each side wants to scare the other more than they want to learn what's really inside these places."

I laughed. "You make it sound like there's some kind of conspiracy, like both the University and the Monastery want to delude everyone..."

His gaze remained stern.

I ceased my laughing and gulped.

"So, um," I searched for an appropriate topic. "Have you chosen yet? University or Monastery?"

"Monastery," Stok said quietly.

"Is that what you want, or your parents?"

A pause. He gazed out beyond the river. "I get to choose."

"Ah."

Stok turned and grinned at me. "I can tell, Le."

"Huh?"

"You're like me."

I stuffed my hands under my legs. "I thought that was obvious."

He laughed. It felt good seeing him smile. "Not that. Well, that too, I guess. What I mean is, you want both. University *and* Monastery. But our system won't let us choose that. They're supposed to be binary. Either or. Science on one side. Religion on the other. Two separate, conflicting ways of understanding the world."

"Aren't they though?"

Stok shook his head. "They're... different paths to the same unreachable thing. Most people are content to take just one of the paths laid out before them. I want to try them all... then make my own."

He reached out, extending his hand toward one of the nanite lumens. It glowed brighter, and he drew it in.

He snatched it, and I jumped. My heart fluttered.

He pushed the fist into my chest, then opened his

palm. The light burst forth into an electric haze, illuminating his eyes.

The next thing I knew, I held him in my arms, and we kissed.

I'd only been inside the Monastery a couple of times before. Huge columns of stone adorned its walls. Cardra incense slammed into my nostrils in waves, each seeming to steal a bit of my consciousness as it wafted away. It was as though the whole building was pulsating, alive in a way that other structures weren't.

Alongside me strode Tully.

She was a tall woman, probably in her early thirties. Her skin was lighter than most. She wore glasses, and her hair was held together in a swirling bun. She walked very precisely, as though each step were sacred.

I tried to mimic her movements at first, but failed, and decided to just try and walk as politely as I could instead.

Her rigid posture and hostile air put me instantly on guard. I usually got along well with women. This Tully... I didn't know what to make of her.

The Monastery interiors were huge, but the footfalls of our bare feet resounded only the faintest of echoes about the space.

Tully had stopped me from entering when I'd first arrived.

"Book of Penitence, Chapter 5, Verse 16." She tapped a button on her computer, and holographic projection of the Writ appeared in the air. "And in the great places of the Divine One, no soul shall bear any cloth made of animal remains, nor of fibrous plants."

The projection faced me, apparently for my unenlightened benefit. Tully clearly had the passage memorized.

I raised my eyebrows a bit. "You're not asking me to undress...?"

"Just your sandals, Initiate Le."

"Why are we following just part of the rule?"

She pursed her lips and he eyes bulged a bit.

I removed my sandals.

The two of us walked and walked. Both the Monastery and University made claim to the same title of grandest structure in River Province, the pinnacle of Alterran architecture.

We passed a mural depicting the creation story I'd helped recite in class just yesterday. The Divine One was always portrayed as a dark-skinned man, reaching down from the clouds. My parents spoke frequently about the sad fact that some people still thought the Divine One actually was some kind of man-figure living in the sky.

"What metaphors does this story employ?" Mom had instructed me when we'd read the Writ together. "What's the moral of this story? Do you agree with it?"

I wondered just then if this Tully had ever found the metaphors.

We passed a room with strong, iron locks over its door, a column of a dozen or more of them sealing the entrance,

Blue light emanated from between the door and its frame, its intensity oscillating.

The portal.

Tully turned and glared at me. I thought she might actually grab me, so I hurried away from the blue glow.

"Do not stray," she said.

"Yes, ma'am."

She led me into a room on the far side of the Monastery, small and lined with bookshelves. She sat down at a desk, and I took the chair facing it. Had it been built for small children? My butt barely fit, and its seat was too low to the ground, my knees nearly jabbing my chest.

Tully glared down at me, and I crossed my arms.

"Do you understand the weight of this decision, Initiate Le?"

I nodded. "Yes, Master Tully."

She jabbed a button on her computer. "High marks in physics, chemistry, mathematics, computer science. Mediocre grades in literature, philosophy, history and languages."

Her eyes peeked out over the rim of her glasses. Anger welled up within me. I could study all those subjects just fine, I'd just been advised not to by "well meaning" people like my boyfriend. I tried to keep control of my emotions. I knew better, I really did, but kind words eluded me. "So being smart means I can't be interested in the Divine One?"

"I'm just suggesting, Initiate Le, that perhaps you

aren't being entirely honest with the Monastery. I don't think you understand all the implications of your behaviors."

I raised an eyebrow. I nearly stood, but I knew that insubordination would seal the deal. I'd never get into Monastery. I'd never see *him* again.

"The Monastery has engineers and scientists," I sighed. "Monktech needs maintenance too."

Tully pressed buttons on her computer. "Initiate Le. Do you have anything you can show me that would suggest that you would be anything other than a mediocre disciple? Are your parents active in religious life? Are your friends? Do you take part in weekly ritual? Anything?"

"I want to learn," I said. That was true. "Relentlessly."

"Wanting is one thing." Tully squared her shoulders. "Performing is another."

She pressed a button, and a hologram of my application appeared over her desk. A red glow seeped in from the edges, absorbing it until the whole document hung in the air like a giant, bloody stain.

"I afraid I have to recommend that, should you choose Monastery, you will begin at the remedial level. Until your comprehension of the core curriculum is up to snuff."

I glared at her. My chest heaved up at down.

She shot me a dangerous look. "Will there be anything else, Initiate Le?"

"No," I mumbled and bit my lip.

We walked to the main foyer in awkward silence. She

left me without another word.

The wind whipped up as I put my sandals back on and exited the Monastery. The sun was high in the sky. I burst into a sweat the moment I stepped beneath its gaze. Even at this elevation, it was hot. It'd be miserable down by the river. Dad was tending today. I should head home, maybe help mom with errands before dinner—

My handy buzzed. I was only halfway down the hill. The Monastery loomed over me.

I sighed and tapped it.

"Le?"

"Hi, Shey." Still failing at sounding happy. Or kind. A gross feeling welled up within me. I'd tell him tonight. I had to.

"So, um, did you finish the math homework?"

"No."

"It's due tomorrow."

I pinched the bridge of my nose. "Then I'll do it tonight."

"Come over, Le. I-I missed you... when you disappeared last night."

Guilt slammed into my gut like a sack of jaga roots.

"I'm sorry, Shey. I just... I don't like Resurgence meetings."

"Can we talk about it? Tonight? I'll cook."

I quirked my eyebrows. In the two years I'd known Shey, he'd never cooked. Or even mentioned it.

"That—" I tried to consider my next words carefully,

but they came tumbling out unimpeded by rational thought. "—sounds nice."

"See you at six." A tinge of worry in his voice.

I let my hand slide over the rest of my face.

Shey's cooking was terrible. The sprouts were soggy and he undercooked the rayak meat. The middle was still orange.

I at least found it easy to feign delight at his cooking. He must have spent a small fortune on the cider. I found myself wondering how many hours of his part time job in the lab that small, ornate bottle represented.

After we'd finished eating, he smiled at me. All of my trepidation, my guilt, my inability to pretend came rushing back. I shifted my weight.

Shey's smile flattened and he grabbed up the plates. I tried to help, but he held out his hand. "Why don't you get out our math homework while I clean up?"

I nodded and fetched my computer from my bag, which I'd left near the front door. Shey's family lived in a big house. They had three stories, bigger than most other houses in Rig. Probably the rest of River Province. I'd never been to Yajur or Sama, but Shey's family probably lived well by their standards, too. His dad was a House of Analytics rep, someone I avoided interaction with at all costs. He often just glared at me, his face flat and unreadable. Uncomfortably morose. And the things he said to Shey when he did speak...

I snatched up my computer and took it to the living room where I sat down at a small table in the corner. I pushed the button on the little lamp, and a dim illumination splayed across the yellow, finished surface.

Memories surged back to me. Shey's and my first kiss had been at this table, in just this dim glow. Days of studying together in the Bibliotech, learning how to code together, and he'd been the first to summon up the nerve to ask me if I'd like to study at his place. He'd leaned over and kissed me.

A barrage of emotions swirled within me. All that happiness, mixed with frustration and the guilt... the guilt in particular tightened into a sickening knot in my stomach.

I turned off the light and snatched up my computer.

The room's main lighting burst on.

Shey stood in the doorway.

"Le?"

"Shey—"

Shey walked to me. My feet seemed glued to the floor. He put his hand on my hip.

"Le, what's wrong?"

I opened my mouth. I had to tell him. I had to tell him.

"I went into a zone." Not what I had quite intended to say, but I supposed it was a start.

"You... *what?*" Shey jerked his hand away and stumbled backward. His back hit the doorframe and he grabbed it for support.

I took a deep breath.

"Have you been to a doctor?" Shey asked. "When did this happen?"

"Yesterday."

"My *Logic*, Le. The code in there is centuries old."

"Shey, I'm fine."

Shey's face flushed red and he bunched up his fists. *"Have you been to a doctor?"*

"No, Shey. I know how to run a nanogenic scan on myself. I don't need a doctor for that!"

Shey gaped and shook his head. "The nanites must be hiding. They've got ways of eluding basic scans. What if they're affecting your musculature, or your *brain*? You need a medical professional—"

Rage boiled up within me. "No, I don't!"

"What if they quarantine you?" Tears welled up in his eyes.

I scoffed, snatched up my computer, ran out of the living room, hurtled through the kitchen, and threw open the door to the back patio. The ebbing dry heat of night blasted into me.

A hand caught my bicep and turned me around.

"Le." Shey streamed tears. "I love you."

My response rang out clearly in my mind. I knew I needed to say it, but images of Shey crumpling to the ground assaulted my mind. I imagined emotional pain, depression and regret sending him into a downward spiral, an unending abyss. I couldn't say the words. Divine One help me, I couldn't say them.

I shrugged off his hand, and I ran. My sandals clapped against the stone. My eyesight blurred. I turned and rounded Zone A. The University peeked over the walls. The metallic slabs gave way to the impressive mud-brick fortification surrounding the University campus in the shape of a perfectly equilateral triangle.

I screamed and hurled my computer at the facade. Glass and metal exploded on impact, and I took off running.

To the river.

I careened into the Zone H wall, the place where Stok had pulled me inside the day before, and I collapsed. The sizzling of a spark burst sounded over my head, and I cried.

I felt a force at my back.

I scrambled to a stance, and the wall opened up. Stok's face appeared between the slabs, a smirk creep out of the edges of his lips.

My tears ceased.

"You came back," Stok said.

I managed a nod. Stok ushered me inside and drew the wall closed behind me. The lights danced even more gloriously than the night before.

Stok walked to me, very slowly. He tried to put his arms around me, but I grabbed his shoulders and held him at arm's length.

Words still eluded me. I just stood, gasping for breath, my eyes undoubtedly red.

Stok gulped. "Is it... Shey?"

I nodded weakly. "I couldn't do it. I wasn't strong enough."

Stok frowned and nodded.

"And the Monastery." I threw up my arms. "They said that if I joined, I'd have to start at remedial. I mean, I can't say I blame them. As long as I can remember, everyone's just assumed I'd go to University. I never thought to try harder in the classes the University doesn't care about." I looked directly into Stok's eyes. "You make me want something different. Something new. Not Monastery or University. I want to learn all about that. What else is there?"

Stok's smile returned, brighter than before, amplified by the sizzle of two colliding nanite lumens. He clasped my hand in his and we took off through the dense forest.

"Last night," Stok began. "When you came into the zone. Do you remember what you were thinking?"

I pondered it over.

"I'm not sure I was thinking anything. It was... impulsive."

"You're on track for University." Stok smirked as he pulled away a mossy branch for me to pass. "What do they teach you about the zones in your science classes?"

"The avatars," I said, "who came to Alterra four hundred years ago, most of them were theologians. They didn't understand nanotechnology very well. So, the nanites that they didn't know how to reprogram or shut down they quarantined in the zones, for everyone's safety. People like the Resurgents want to take over the zones and study the nanites, but the Monastery and the House of Souls won't let them."

"Sounds reasonable." Stok and I began the upward climb. "Would you like to hear what they say in religion and literature and art classes?"

"What's that?"

"That we keep the zones sealed because our modern technozealots would run rampant with nanotechnology if they got their hands on it. Alterra would be overrun with unfeeling, uncaring, life-destroying technology, just like our ancestors worried would happen on Asura."

The trees fell away, and we came to a halt atop the rise that overlooked the river. The waters burbled and churned below us. Green-blue lights danced in the night-cool air.

"Do you think that would happen?" I asked.

Stok shook his head. "No. Both sides have their fringe fanatics, but the vast majority doesn't really want strife. I just worry... the fanatics seem to be getting louder, more powerful. Have you heard of 'The Holy Way?'"

"Sounds familiar."

Stok rolled his eyes. "They're the Monastery analogue to the Resurgence. They think they're some kind of secret society, but everyone in River Province has at least heard whispers of them."

A breeze hit us, blowing all the glowing lights briefly to the right, and I laughed. I smiled, then remembered Shey and promptly frowned.

"Le?"

"Yeah?"

"What were you thinking when you entered the zone last night?"

I shook my head and shrugged.

Stok nodded to the river. "Jump with me."

"Wh-what?!"

Stok squeezed my hand. "Jump with me."

"That's— that's at least fifty meters! And the rocks—"

Stok pressed a finger to my lips. "Don't feel. Don't think."

He pulled me to the precipice. I pulled back. His hand jerked away, out of mine and he fell over the side of the cliff, perfectly calm.

I scrambled to the edge. "*Stok!*"

I watched in horrified silence. Everything else seemed to crystallize around him as he tumbled downward.

Just as he neared the water lapping up against jagged rocks, a blue haze appeared over the river. It engulfed him, and his descent slowed. He came to stop, hovering just above the surface of the water.

He looked up at me and winked.

I took a deep breath and sprang over the edge.

A dim giddiness filled me as I fell. The blue glow caught me too, and I slowed to a halt, just beside Stok. I stretched my foot down, and my toe grazed the surface of the river. My sandal fell off and disappeared into the water with a plop. Stok chuckled and I shot him a snide grin

I shook my head. "This place is amazing. Why are we afraid of all this?"

"Blindness. Neither side is interested in investigating truth anymore, only demonizing their opposition."

I sighed. "I guess I failed your test."

Stok shook his head. "It wasn't a test."

He tried for my hand again. I gave it to him. He wrapped me in his arms as we floated in the air, and I embraced him back.

"You asked me about an alternative to the philosophies of University and Monastery," Stok said. "Here it is: You feel, but you don't feel. You think, but you don't think. And then you jump."

I shook my head. "That doesn't make any sense."

Stok smirked. "Don't worry. You'll figure it out. And then we'll jump together."

I went home feeling oddly invigorated. My problems with Shey seemed universes away. My thoughts swirled around Stok and what he had told me.

Not to think. Not to feel. Just to jump.

I found myself wondering if Stok had indeed known that the riverbank had a layer of anti-grav nanites.

I entered my house through the back door. The living room was a familiar sight—dad with a book and mom at her sculpting table. They looked up and smiled at me.

"How was your dinner?" Dad asked.

"Good," I lied.

Dad's eyes glimmered. "You want to talk about it, son?"

"No." I ran upstairs before he or Mom could continue.

I collapsed onto my bed and pulled the sheets over my head.

My door opened.

"Le?" It was Dad.

"Yeah, Dad?"

"Things aren't going well with Shey, are they?"

"No."

"You want to talk about it?"

"No."

"Le." I recognized that tone. Talk about it or else. Fine.

I pulled myself out of bed and put my feet on the floor. I cradled my head in my hands. "You went to University and mom went to Monastery."

"That's right." Dad shrugged. "Are you saying you want to go to Monastery instead?"

"And what if I said..." I gulped. "That I didn't want to enroll at either?"

Dad raised his eyebrows. He definitely hadn't expected that.

"I—" He paused, took and breath, and seemed to consider his next words carefully. I thought he might just stare at the wall with a disappointed look on his face, but then finally he continued. "I'd want to know that you had a plan. That you want to contribute something to society. That you'd be safe. And happy."

I stood and hugged him. "Thank you, dad."

"What's this about, Le?"

"University... the Resurgence... Dad, what they want is wrong!"

Dad put a hand on my shoulder and we sat down on the edge of my bed.

"The Resurgence isn't the same thing as the University. Not nearly. They're not even a majority. Most people aren't like that."

"Shey is."

"Then you need to tell him how you feel."

I shook my head. "It'll break his heart."

"He deserves to know."

"Monastery isn't for me either, though."

Dad nodded. "That'll be a hard path."

I looked at him, wondering if he'd change his mind.

"If you can find a way to make it work," he said, "you'll have my support. But you don't have long. Just a week 'til the Harvest Festival, right?"

I frowned. "Yeah."

"You'll think of something." Dad winked. "Get some sleep."

I lay in bed. Thoughts of working within the rules to attend neither University nor Monastery occupied my waking thoughts, eventually giving way to dreams of running off into the desert with Stok as I drifted into slumber.

The next few days passed uneventfully. I sat through

classes and went through all the motions, but my heart wasn't in it. School was winding down, anyway. A test here or there was all that stood between us and the Festival. The day after, we'd elect either University or Monastery, and that decision would affect the rest our lives.

I avoided Shey as much as possible. A few times he turned toward my desk just as the bell rang, but I hurried out of the classroom before he had a chance to talk to me. Despite Dad's suggestion, I couldn't face him.

And yet, the next two nights, without fail, I met Stok in Zone H after sunset. We talked for hours, about life, about science, about philosophy, about religion. I shared my love of math and computers, while Stok shared with me the thoughts, values, and ideas of Alterran philosophers of the past four centuries and the Asuran philosophers before them.

I dove beyond the surface of a history I'd only skimmed prior, because I had just assumed that fleshing out such knowledge wouldn't be important for me in my University career. Nothing in the sterile, mathematical world I'd inhabited could compare to what Stok offered. A new kind of science formed in my mind that I hadn't been able to see prior—a science of the human condition. Those nights became a blur, a smear of philosophizing, technowizardry and lovemaking amongst the dancing lights and sizzling sparks of nanite lumens.

Three days after dinner with Shey, I got a text message on my handy from Fera, the woman I'd met at the

Resurgence meeting. The next day was a freeday, and she asked to meet me for lunch. I accepted.

The meeting place she suggested was a teahouse on her side of Rig. It was a quiet place, the walls lined with wooden boxes. Each had a lid flap that you could open and scoop out dried leaves.

You could make a lot of complaints about this valley in terms of human habitability. Diversity of native flora was not one of them.

I made myself tea, ordered a sandwich and took a seat at the table in the center of the room. Fera arrived not long afterward.

She shot me a smile, ordered for herself, and joined me.

I smiled back.

"How are things?" I asked.

"Good. You?"

I couldn't help myself. The last four days came spilling out of me: meeting Stok after dropping her off at home, the disastrous dinner, Stok jumping from the cliff, and seeing him every night thereafter. But also, my secret worry—the Festival was just over a week away, and I still had no plan, no choice besides University or Monastery.

I caught a glint in Fera's eye. "What is it?" I asked.

"Just what I came to tell you about. You're going to love this." She turned on her computer. A document appeared, filled with dense paragraphs of tiny text. The title read, 'University Adjunct Application: Atharva Expedition.'

"The University wants to find the mouth of the Great River. They think there will be a delta."

"Of course," I said. "It'd be even better than the valley."

"Here's the best part." Fera raised her eyebrows. "The terms of the adjunct position don't require you to enroll in University. It makes sense. They're going to need fifty to a hundred people, and they can't spare that many candidates without compromising research—"

"So they're leaving it open to everyone." My heart raced. I felt giddy.

"Which means," Fera continued, "after a two year expedition with all my living expenses paid, I'll be three short months away from being twenty-one years old."

"You can override your parents' wishes."

"And you could get *two years* to figure things out. Hell, Stock might even want to go himself."

I must have been grinning ear to ear. "Oh, if he wants to..."

Fera snatched up her computer. "I'll send you the application."

My parents would let me go for sure, but I didn't have enough information to guess at what Stok would do. Would he want to go, too? I'd learned a lot about how he thought and what his interests were, but spending two years together was another thing entirely from meeting secretly every night.

"I heard the strangest rumor the other day," Fera mentioned. "Maybe Stok mentioned something about it. I'm sure you've heard of the Holy Way by now."

"Sure," I said. "Everyone has."

"Well, I heard that they're going to get a Messenger appointed this year."

I furrowed my brow and pulled my head back. "I'd remember him mentioning that. There hasn't been a Messenger in over a century."

"The rumor is that the Holy Way has convinced a few powerful members of the House of Souls to revive the practice."

I shook my head. "No one will tolerate it... will they? Reminds me of something Stok said. One side gets more dogmatic, so the other side responds by getting more dogmatic. An endless feedback loop."

"Charming fellow." Fera sipped her tea, leveling a sarcastic gaze over the cup.

"Very charming, I'll have you know."

Fera inhaled sharply and pursed her lips. "Steals you into a forest full of centuries-old microscopic computers that do Divine-One-knows-what and jumps off a cliff."

I bunched up my own lips. "Yes. Charming."

We shared a small laugh, and then continued our conversation for another hour or so. One thought nagged at me from the back of my mind the entire time. Would Stok want to go on the expedition, or would he insist on enrolling in Monastery instead?

There was only one way to find out.

—

I sat in my bedroom the rest of the freeday.

My thoughts drifted back to Stok with such frequency that I found I couldn't concentrate on anything. I felt I should have been doing something—running, lifting, swimming, studying—anything except what I did. I watched the sun set. Boiling kettles have absolutely nothing on the rotation of our planet.

At one point, mom came up and tried to talk to me. I barely remembered the interaction afterward, like it was part of some dream I'd had the night before.

When the sun finally dipped below the towering dune in the western sky, another arduous wait began. The sky turned crimson, then violet, then ran through various shades of yellow and brown and finally, finally to black. It seemed to take even longer for the glow in the twilight sky to dim.

I paced.

I did push-ups. Then sit-ups.

When I couldn't take it anymore, I ran out the back door and did a lap around the entire circumference of my neighborhood.

Still a haze of light in the western sky. The stars remained dim.

I grimaced through my sweat and ran to the edge of the city. I ran past the limits, out onto the dusty road that followed the river south to Sama. A car's headlights appeared in the distance, and I ran toward the river.

The ground grew reedy and wet, the sand giving way

to mud. I tore off my wickshirt, my sandals and my shorts, and I dove into the river. The water was cold, but my heart raced and my skin burned rapturously. The current pulled me along, and I added all my strength, swimming as hard as I could through the night.

Between strokes I caught the hoarse croaks of gemma toads, and I imagined that they were cheering me on.

I swam and swam and before long, the wall of Zone H appeared along the shore. I was gasping for every breath, but I pushed myself faster still.

When I felt myself grow lighter and my arms started skipping above the surface of the water, I pulled my head up and watched as my body rise out of the river, dripping beads of water and bathed in blue light. Laughter tumbled out of me.

"Le?" An incredulous voice from above.

I spotted Stok on the precipice.

"Jump!" I called out through my laughter.

His form hurtled toward me, and I reached out, wrapping my arms around him as he fell into me.

Stok grinned and shook his head. "You *swam* here?"

I nodded.

"You're insane."

"Maybe." I bit my lip. "Stok, I—I want to talk about something."

I sat down cross-legged, albeit floating in the air, and pulled Stok down. He sat across from me.

I cleared my throat and wrapped his hands in mine. "If

you go to Monastery and I go to University, we'll hardly ever see each other. Today, I found out about something. It's called the Atharva Expedition. The University wants to find the river delta. It'll take two years. Everyone's welcome, especially the uninitiated. The University wants to keep most of its candidates at home, of course.

"Stok—" Words caught in my throat, but I swallowed hard. This was too important a moment to wuss out. "Stok, these last five days, spending time with you, it's amazing. *You're* amazing. I want to be with you. I want to give us a chance. We could go on the expedition together. We'll worry about University and Monastery when we get back."

Stok smiled calmly. I looked away and fidgeted with my hands, worried he didn't like the idea, that our conversations hadn't meant as much to him as they did to me. Maybe I was just some trick in the woods.

He wrapped his hands around mine and squeezed. "First, I have to tell you what I'm worried about. I'm sure they're making a big show of being 'open' to everyone, but I think that really, anyone who studied for Monastery is going to be treated as a second class citizen. And why do you think they want to find the delta, anyway?"

I shrugged. "Who wouldn't want to?"

Stok eyed me. "I think they want to move the University there eventually."

I blinked a few times. "Hmm. I guess... the University and Monastery might fight less?"

Stok shook his head. "They'll fight more. The Monastery can't move because of the portal. If the University relocates, Rig's intellectual potential will wither. And this new 'Atharva' delta would find itself home to a city rich in technological marvels, but lacking in compassion, in ethics, in human spirit. The answer's not to separate the University and Monastery, or escape from them. It's to put them together. And then discover all the different institutions and worldviews that don't exist, because humans haven't thought of them yet."

I looked down at the water lapping at my feet. My heart plunged into that frigid, flowing mass.

"Le?"

I looked up. Stok was smiling.

"I'll go."

I beamed, lurched forward, and tackled him. We rolled toward the river. The blue glow dissipated and we fell, splashing into the water.

We laughed out air bubbles. I pulled at him and we swam back to shore where I helped him out of his soaking wet clothes.

I stifled tears. "Why?"

"Because I like our talks. Because you're smart. And because you do things like swim down rivers at night mostly naked when you could have just walked into the zone."

I grinned and pulled him closer. "Stok... I love you."

"I love you too, Le."

—

"Le!" Shey stood in the door frame, his mouth open. His face laid his emotions plainly before me. Sadness and regret oozed off him, draining the color from everything nearby.

"Hi, Shey."

He opened the door further. "Come inside."

"Okay."

I stepped into the foyer. I could hear his mother and sister moving and talking in the kitchen. Shey led me upstairs to his room, a large space with a pair of windows, one facing east toward the river and the other north. Three computer banks lined the walls, their surfaces covered with holographic projections.

The order degraded outward from the computers. Clothes lay strewn about the floor. His bed was a mess. And now that I could see him better, his hair was unkempt too, and he had dark circles under his eyes.

He motioned for me to sit on the bed. I did.

He sat down next to me. He put his hand on my thigh and I flinched. Couldn't help it.

Despair erupted from him and he slunk back.

"Shey, I—"

"Le—"

We both began at the same time. He motioned for me to go ahead.

"Shey, I need to tell you something. I've decided to sign up for the Atharva Expedition."

He creased his brow. "You mean... the search for the delta?"

I nodded.

He shook his head. "Le, they're not going to need brains on an expedition. They're looking for grunts. You can achieve so much more. Is this what's been bothering you? Enrollment at the University? I can't imagine your grades are bad."

"My grades are fine."

He clasped my shoulder, his eyes searching mine. "Then why?"

"I wish I could explain to you... philosophy, art, literature and religion, they have a place—"

Shey dropped his hand from my shoulder. He turned away and scoffed.

I snarled. "They have a place in our society! An important place!"

"You would turn your back on science and the University. The Monastery doesn't give a damn about progress or innovation."

"Science is *not* the only thing that matters."

"It is the *only* thing that has ever mattered for the quality of human life."

I stood up and looked down at him. "The Resurgence is wrong, Shey!"

He stood up, returning my stare. "Fine. You want to go to the Monastery? You want to throw your life away reciting chants and speaking to some childish delusion of a person in the sky so you can feel better about your mortality? You go do that. The rest of us will make this world something we can be proud of. You know, we had a progressive, prosperous world once. It was called Asura. And our idiotic, *braindead* ancestors were so stubbornly against science and progress that they got themselves *kicked out*. And here we are, four hundred years later, and we still haven't learned. Because of people like you."

My heart surged within my chest. I clenched my fists. His room glowed red. "You are such an arrogant, self-important ass sometimes, Shey!"

Shey took a step back. A new look came over his eyes. "Who's been feeding you this nonsense?"

"No one." I bunched my lips. I tried to keep my features level, to calm my temper, but I must have let it slip.

Shey's eyes widened, enraged. "*Who is he?*"

"None of your damn business! We're over, Shey!" I marched out of his room.

A hand grabbed my shoulder and I threw it off.

"Wait, Le—!"

"Save it!" I didn't look back.

"Please, Le. I didn't mean it. I'm sorry."

He must have remained at the top of the stairs. I didn't look back.

I exited the house and broke into a run. I ran all the way back home, faster and faster.

I careened through the back door—my parents a blur streaking the kitchen. They said some things I didn't comprehend, and I babbled back something incoherent. I hurtled up the stairs, into my room, where I collapsed onto my bed and bawled my eyes out.

Mom and Dad drifted in and out of my room throughout the afternoon. They said all the things they could think of to make me feel better. "Grunt work? The nerve! I wish they'd had an expedition when I was nineteen!" "Science is the only thing that improves our lives? That's pretty extreme."

They reminded me of all the things about the Atharva Expedition I was avoiding thinking about, too. "I know you don't want to hear this, Le, but have you thought about what would happen if your relationship with this Stok fellow soured on the trip? Would you still be able to work with him every day?"

It seemed so unreal. I'd been dragging my knees through a river of sludge and not even known it. Stok had lifted me from that quagmire and shown me a glimpse of a world I'd only dreamed existed. My feelings for him were genuine and mutual, weren't they?

"Why don't you invite Stok over for dinner tonight?" Dad suggested.

I sat up straight in my bed. I turned to him. "Yeah." I muttered the word, realization washing over me.

I looked out the window. The sun was low in the sky. In my grief, I'd forgotten I was now free. Stok and I no longer required our relationship to be hidden. He'd told me where he lived, of course, but I'd never been there.

I lurched out of bed, hugged my father, and ran out of the room. His hearty laughter trailed behind me. I first went to the bathroom and cleaned up my face. I adjusted my wickshirt, which had gotten bunched up in my hours of keeping myself bedridden.

I rushed downstairs and out the door into the dry streets of Rig. I took off to the south.

Zone D, Zone D.

Where was that again?

Zone A appeared, and the top of the University beyond it.

West. Zone D should be west of here. I turned and followed the setting sun. I veered slightly north up a rise, so I could get a better view. I crested the hill. Clusters of trees and tall, curving still grass dotted the city, each surrounded by twisting, gray slabs of metal.

I ticked off the zones with my eyes. "B, C, D!"

I took off down the hill toward it.

The sunlight began to wane.

No, don't let it get too late. He might leave for the zone.

My stomach growled, and my frustration peaked.

Which house was his? They all looked the same. This was one of the poorer regions of the city, the houses all single story rectangles with flat roofs.

Thirty-five. He said thirty-five. But which street?

The sun grew dimmer.

Fed up, I ran to a door and knocked.

"Is Stok at home?"

Wrong address.

I ran to house thirty-five on the next street.

Wrong again.

On the third try an elderly man answered the door. I said Stok's name meekly, and to my surprise, the old man smiled.

He turned around. "Stok? You've got a visitor." He turned back to me. "What's your name, son?"

"Le," I said.

Stok careened out the door and grabbed me up in his arms. "Le!"

"It's so good to see you!" His embrace was bliss. We stood on his porch in the last glimpses of daylight, the old man smiling brightly.

"Le," Stok turned to him. "This is my grandfather."

"Hi," I said. "Um, Master Thiksay."

The old man grinned. "Just 'Arnalt' will do fine."

My face flushed red. "Oh, uh, really? Are you sure?"

"'Course I'm sure!" He disappeared into the house.

Stok nudged me with his elbow. "Gramps has funny ideas about hierarchies. Says they're 'inherently toxic.' Doesn't like honorifics."

I smiled. "I... could get used to that."

"C'mon." Stok tugged at my sleeve.

Arnalt gave me a glass of water, and Stok showed me around his house. We stopped outside his bedroom, his grandfather's, then the combination kitchen and living room. A trampoline lay beyond the screen door to the back yard, a solitary island in a sea of yellow sand.

Bookshelves lined every available wall. In my house, dad's library occupied the basement. Here, though, it was as if their study had erupted and encased Stok's entire home. Every vertical surface that wasn't a closet or doorway was lined with shelving. Stacks of books lay about the floor too, piled up in neat little columns.

I spotted one empty shelf in the living room. A single item adorned the space, a photo. It stood out so starkly against the sea of books, that I had to lean in for a closer look. The photo showed a smiling, five-year-old Stok with his mother, father, and all four grandparents.

"My parents died when I was nine," Stok said from behind me, and I started.

I turned to him, and searched his eyes, but their usual light was absent. Only dark black embers lay there, and his face dipped toward the floor.

"Stok, I—"

"It's okay. You don't have to be sorry." He smiled weakly. "I have Grandpa. And I remember them. It's okay."

Not knowing what else to do, I wrapped my arms around him. He shuddered a bit, and I held him tighter.

He sniffled and pulled away.

I took his hand and led him to the kitchen where his grandfather stood, chopping vegetables.

"Mast— Arnalt," I said. "Can Stok come to my house for dinner tonight? My parents would like to meet him."

Arnalt replied with a bemused grin. "Only if you will allow us to extend you the same courtesy tomorrow."

"That's Grandpa for 'yes'," Stok whispered in my ear.

"I heard that, young man." Arnault smirked. "I'm not deaf yet."

"I'd love that," I said. "Thank you, Arnault."

"You're welcome. And try to be home by a decent hour! I can't stay up as late as I used to..."

We said goodbye to Arnault and left Stok's house. Our hands found one another's and we proceeded through the streets of Rig in the twilight.

The air felt frenetic with possibility. Being with Stok felt right. I had never felt more alive.

I got steadily more tense as we approached my house. I must have been walking robotically when I opened my front door for him, but by the time we sat down for dinner I felt oddly relaxed. From the moment he'd introduced himself, Stok had a rapport with both my mom *and* my dad. A little part of me begrudgingly remembered Shey, who'd always been so awkward around my mom, never knowing quite what to say, maintaining his distance with affected politeness. Stok got everyone laughing in a way that felt genuine.

He asked my mom about the Monastery and my dad about the University. He got them to tell the story about how they'd met on the intramural Rig voidball team. I think he shot me a wry look at that point, as if to say, "your own parents graduated from different institutions, you kook!"

After dinner, he helped my dad clean up the table while I made tea with my mom in the kitchen. Mom even got out her stash of Yajur sweet biscuits and we indulged in the flaky confections over tea.

Dad nodded and smiled as I led Stok out the door. The night air was cool, even damp. A light wind drifted over us from the direction of the river, and the stars were bright in the sky.

"You make a lot more sense now," Stok said.

"Oh yeah?"

"Your parents are both like you. Your dad, the chemical researcher by day who spends his nights reading novels, who can talk about all the major Alterran literary movements. And your mom, the artist, whose work is geometrical and precise, like she's carving up the world into discreet, perfectly articulated segments."

I grinned, sheepishly I think. "I never really thought about my family that way."

He gave my hand a gentle squeeze. "I never thought I would meet anyone else who can see multiple perspectives like this. And I definitely never thought this would happen. I'm happy it did."

"Me too."

We arrived at his home, and I stopped outside his front door. "Well, um... I guess this is good night..."

His eyes lit up. "You want to stay a while?"

I blushed. "Well, yeah, but, um, with your grandfather here..."

Stok chuckled and slapped me on the shoulder. He grabbed my hand and pulled me toward his house. We entered. Seeing his grandson home safe and sound, Arnault thanked me for having Stok over.

"We're going to use the trampoline for a bit," Stok said.

Arnault mumbled something of an affirmative and shuffled away toward his bedroom.

The back door squeaked as we opened it and slammed shut as we retreated away from the bright lights of the kitchen into the relative darkness of the trampoline. Behind Stok's backyard, a few other properties could be seen, but mostly the dunes rose up into a wall of sand not more than a few hundred meters away.

We climbed up over the metal frame and onto the stretchy material.

Stok bounced on both feet and surged into the air. He launched upward and back down. On his fourth jump, I caught him as he came down. We laughed, and then both started jumping as high as we could go together. We caught each other in the air and bounced on and on into the night.

Jumping gave way to conversation, an activity we fell into easily.

I sat on the stretchy fabric with Stok's head in my lap, running my fingers through his hair.

Worry overcame me and I gulped. "Stok?"

"Yeah?"

"I didn't know about your family when I asked you to... Anyway, I'd understand if you have to stay for your grandpa."

"'Cuz he'd be all alone?"

"Yeah."

He nodded a little. He reached up and ran the back of his hand over my cheek. "I talked to him about it, actually. He says he'll be okay. I don't think he'd be overjoyed to see me go, but I'm tempted to believe him. He's pretty active in the Monastery community. We've always had people who care about our family."

"Are you sure?"

"Yeah." He cringed and let out a small laugh. "He started trying to tell me about when he was nineteen."

I chuckled. "Say no more."

Stok gulped. "Though..."

"What is it?"

He looked up into my eyes. "I'm actually more worried about what the Monastery and University are going to be like when we get back. Right now it's just talk, but I feel people getting more hostile, more divided. Does that void-ball team exist anymore, the one where your parents met?"

"No," I admitted.

Stok pulled himself up and sat beside me. "And my other worry..."

"What is it?"

He took a deep sigh and gulped. "The truth is... I feel like I've been lying to you. I just happened into a zone one day. By accident. And I knew about the anti-grav nanites, of course. I don't have ancient wisdom, and I can't code worth a damn. I'm just good enough with computers to type reports for Religion class. I think you think I'm someone special... but I'm just a regular guy."

I grabbed up his hands, and shook my head back and forth. "The way you see things, Stok... Before I met you, I had no idea I could even consider anything besides University! You... you showed me how to look at *all* the possibilities, not just the ones sitting in front of me. That make you special to me."

He bunched up his face into a small smile. "Really? That's all it takes?"

"Really. Way more than you give yourself credit for."

He tackled me and we rolled around on the trampoline, bouncing a bit. His lips met mine.

"We'll make this work," I said. "No matter what. I want to be with you."

He smiled widely, wrapping me in his arms. "All the new potentials, Le. Let's discover them together. What do you say?"

"Sounds like a plan."

The next few days became a blur. I pushed everything to the periphery of my attention, final exams, chores, my family, everything. Time with Stok became the rhythm of my life.

We would go to his house or mine. When our parents were around, we would sit together and talk, and when alone, we would burst into fits of passion.

The first night his grandfather cooked for us, we found ourselves outside on the trampoline afterward, and we talked about exploring the other zones. Even though Zone H was harmless, Stok had never explored the others, for fear that their nanites might actually be as hazardous as was widely believed.

I took him back to my house and started up the replacement computer dad had begrudgingly bought me after some harsh words. I glanced at Stok between typing, and he smiled, even though he probably had no idea what my code would do.

Once I was reasonably sure my program would work, I rummaged around my closet for my old chemistry set and got out a small, glass petri dish. I blew the dust off it and unscrewed it, then grabbed up the set's scalpel.

Stok stayed my hand. "What are you doing?"

"I'm just going to scrape off a little skin. Nothing to worry about. I need some human DNA, is all."

Stok's eyes were shot through with intensity. "Let me do it."

I dropped my head and narrowed my gaze. "Everything okay?"

"Yeah." Stok grabbed up the scalpel and scraped lightly at the back of his hand over the dish.

I picked up the computer. "Okay. That's it. Plenty of cells. We're good."

I scavenged up my MicroN2 out of the junk heap of my closet. It had been a gift a few years back from my uncle—a computer that was designed to be small instead of powerful. It didn't even have hologenerators. You had to plug it into a regular computer to see any output. But it would suit our present purposes nicely. I cut open the side of the petri dish and fitted the sensor unit of the N2 inside.

"What now?" Stok asked.

I grinned. "Watch."

I uploaded the program I'd written into the N2, executed it, and a dashboard appeared in the air out of my main computer, one which displayed a detailed analysis of state of each of the cells in the petri dish.

"We don't have to go inside ourselves," I said. "Just set this inside and leave it there for a while. If anything in there is toxic or has a taste for human cells, we'll find out."

Stok turned me around and kissed me. "That's hot."

I couldn't help but giggle. "Writing code is hot?"

"Yeah," he whispered in my ear while his hands moved elsewhere.

Things moved to my bed from there.

Once night fell, we snuck out to Zone G, slid a wall slab open just a crack, shoved the N2-petri dish apparatus inside and closed up the wall. The next night we returned and stood outside at the same spot. I used my computer to link wirelessly with the MicroN2 while Stok fidgeted and glanced about.

A grin stretched out on my face, and I moved the holographic display toward him.

"Nothing dangerous?"

I nodded. "Perfectly safe."

We went to zone after zone in a similar manner, night after night, and the results were nothing short of extraordinary. Zone after zone proved safe. The most dangerous part was actually our fellow citizens–fear of being discovered dominated the moments of trying to slip the N2 between wall slabs, especially as we came to Zones A, B, and E, which lay in heavily trafficked parts of the city. We had to walk the circumference of Zone B so many times that Stok worried someone might find our behavior suspicious and pulled me away toward the next zone.

The experiment ended at Zone D. My first indication of trouble was the stench that exuded when we pulled the wall slightly open. When I linked in to the N2 the next night, we discovered that D's nanites were producing elemental chlorine. We abandoned the MicroN2 then and there.

But that still left six other safe Zones for us to explore.

In Zone A, the nanites had grown into paper-thin, gray metallic webs, connecting trees, roots, and vines.

In Zone B, our bodies grew lighter as we entered. Trees towered monumentally above the walls, and huge, thick vines hung suspended in thin air. The spiders and insects had grown massive over the centuries. Their buzzes, burrs, and chirps filled the glade.

In Zone C, the nanites pulled water out of the ground and up the sides of plants, causing it to rain back down from their leaves. The glade gave new meaning to the phrase 'it always sounds like rain near Parliament.' Though intended as a bitter reminder of our ineffectual, perpetually-deadlocked government, the phrase bore some literal truth after all.

As our explorations into the zones grew more intense, the expectations of our participation in the Festival ramped up too, cutting into our free time. My parents took me out to get fitted for a tunic, as did Arnault for Stok. I was compelled by my parents to actually get some voidball practice in, my chosen tournament, though I'd never cared much for any sports. Stok had chosen track six months ago, when all us initiates had decided such things.

He and I anxiously looked up the schedule for voidball and track on our computers, and hugged when we discovered the events were in different time blocks.

Banners and streamers were erected on the great hill around the Monastery, demarcating an area that stretched through the sandy soil, all the way up to the base of the University. The Festival grounds and Parliament were probably the only two connections between those two competitors that remained.

The annual tradition tugged at our hearts harder with each passing day, but we persisted in our nightly adventures. I didn't want to miss a moment with Stok.

I passed Shey once. He entered the bathroom at school just as I was leaving. We regarded each other coldly. His eyes drew all the light out of the room, burning with sadness and anger. Guilt welled up within me, and I shuffled past him as fast as I could.

The moment was forgotten by the time I saw Stok next.

The week was a blur, but Stok stood at the center, stable and clear. He remained unyieldingly loving, and I loved him back.

On the night of the Festival, I went to his house, dressed in my tunic, all gaudy blues and golds with ornate patterns woven into the fabric, some kind of style to signify the year. And now I'd do what I'd seen all the graduates do year after year—roll around in the sand and make the thing filthy.

Stok stepped out from his house alongside Arnault, the light from the doorway framing his body. His tunic clung to him, baggy in some places, but tight in all the right ones. I smiled to him, and he stepped down from his porch. We took each other's hands and walked down the road together, faster than my parents and Arnault, who became enraptured in their own conversation.

"You ready for this?" Stok asked.

My heart was pounding out of my chest. "Are you kidding? Today, we start a two-year adventure. This is going to be the best day of my life."

Stok squeezed my hand and smiled. "You want to

race? To the festival?"

"Careful," I suggested. "Don't use up all your energy before the games."

He winked. "I'll be fine."

"On three," I said.

We dropped to our hands and took off into a sprint toward the Festival grounds, our new shoes kicking up sand in our wake.

We came to a halt at the Festival gates, panting.

I turned to him, gasping for breath. "What do you think? Was that a tie?"

He winked. "I think you got it."

I punched him playfully in the shoulder. "Liar."

A throng of people shuffled through the makeshift entrance before us into the Festival grounds. Monks stood on either side of the gateway, each holding a small monktech cube. Each person held their palm under the cube for the scan, then proceeded inside.

I reached the gate, and held out my hand in turn.

The monk's cube sizzled and shook.

The monk craned his neck down.

"Sorry, master." I wiped my hands on my shorts, and the registration took that time.

Stok grabbed my shoulder and pulled me into the Festival grounds. Blue and yellow streamers rippled in the wind, hanging from enormous metal poles. The area near the gate was crowded with food vendor stalls, and we hurried off toward the University side of the grounds, where the arenas lay.

Blue and yellow fluttered in the air, and I was glad our year had gotten such good colors. Last year had been purple and green. I felt sorry for those poor people whose commencement pictures would forever bear that hideous combination of hues.

We came to the track strip, a stretch of cracked dirt wiped clear of sand. Our peers from school were already lined up at the starting line, stretching. Stok gave me a peck on the lips and ran to the starting line himself.

Arnault approached and stood beside me.

"Hi, Arnault."

He didn't respond, so I looked up at him. He gazed into the distance, beyond the track, frowning.

"Arnault?"

He put his hand on my shoulder. "I'm glad you're here, Le."

I didn't know what to say.

"I just wish my son was here to see his son's commencement games, is all."

I gave Arnault my best smile. Worry struck me momentarily, but then two middle-aged couples approached and struck up a conversation with Arnault, asking all about Stok. Arnault smiled, and the air around him lightened.

A gunshot.

Runners sprinted.

I shouted for Stok alongside Arnault and his friends.

Halfway through the dozen scheduled heats, some of the runners started to lose their shirts. I recognized the guy who started it. A real show off. Braggy, too. I'd never liked him. His behavior was infectious though, spreading to the others.

By the time the eighth sprint started, half the runners were down to shorts and shoes. At the start of the tenth sprint, only Stok still wore his tunic, while every other runner's lay at the starting line.

I caught his eye as he walked back from the eleventh sprint. The facilitator handed him a water tube, and he gulped the liquid down.

He came in eleventh out of twenty-seven.

After the races, I took him to the stands where he inhaled two full plates of Festival food, all of it varying combinations of sugar and fat. I'd never seen him eat so eagerly. He looked up at me when he was done, and caught me grinning at him. We laughed and talked about voidball. He asked who was on my team.

Halfway through my description of the plays we'd planned, Stok's expression abruptly fell and he nodded his head at the space over my left shoulder.

I turned. A man in a blue-grey suit and tie was screaming at a trio of monks by the Festival entrance. On either side of him stood a man and a woman in white laboratory outfits. They were some ways off, and the noise from the nearby tables drowned out the man's voice.

I heard Stok stand up, his chair scraping the ground, and I turned to him. His face was flushed, his eyes scared. I turned back toward the scene, but the irate University contingent had disappeared, presumably back into the crowd. The monks walked back to their posts at the entrance.

"What was that?" I asked Stok.

He shook his head. "I honestly don't know." He lowered his voice. "Scary, though."

Stok was scared? The guy who'd snuck into more than half the zones with me? I gulped and stood up myself. People around us cast us odd looks.

"Stok?"

"I'm fine," he said quietly, and sat down.

I returned to my seat, too.

"Sorry." Stok regained his composure. "You were saying about the other third quarterman?"

I gulped and started in again about my voidball pair. His name was Thondi, and I'd never talked to him much until recently. He was big into sports, particularly voidball, which I'd always found intimidating in and of itself. When I'd found out he was my pair, I wasn't sure what to think.

Our practices had been good, though. He'd instructed me with patience, which I appreciated, but held me at a distance, apprehensive, even disinterested, but never hostile.

I'd told Stok about the time in seventh year, when a voidball second quarterman had trampled me to get the ball into the third quarter instead of passing to me. A thug and a bully, he'd shouted an obscenity as to my sexuality as he'd done it.

My parents had both gone down to the school, and the bully had been suspended from the voidball team for the rest of the year.

It was the first and last time a slur had been directed my way.

Thondi was none of that. He merely cared about the sport more than I did. I think he sensed that for me this was just a rite of passage. It meant more for him. And that was fine for us both.

Stok and I arrived at the voidball court. The lines on the ground painted out the field, a square carved up into four smaller squares of equal size, and each of those cut vertically in half so that each contained an inner triangle and an outer triangle.

Thondi was already in third. He, Ved, Kozh and Naga stood passing the voidball around in a circle, a common warm-up. After eight rotations, they jumped back into the outer tris and our opponents jumped into the inner tris, taking up the ball and practicing the same drill.

I ran up to Thondi and he silently motioned for me to take his place in the warm up. I scanned the sidelines, finding Stok standing alongside my parents and Arnault. I barely jumped into the inner tri in time.

After a few rounds of practice under the hot sun, sweat lines had already formed around the neck of my tunic, and my face had flushed.

A whistle sounded, and all fifteen other players joined me on the field. Another whistle, and the game began.

Our team started on defense. Thondi took the corner, and I played distraction.

The opposing team took the ball easily through first and second quarter. It arrived in the hands of a guy named Munnar, big and stocky. He surged down the second diagonal and hurtled the ball towards third.

Ved, my team's second, corrected almost in time, but the ball grazed his fingertips.

I sprang for it, arms outstretched, contacted the ball and dive-rolled into the outer tri. Stok and my parents shouted my name. My adrenaline surged.

I righted myself and targeted Thondi. He stood ready and I whipped the ball toward him. He altered the ball's trajectory more than caught it, helping it over the corner to Madurai, who passed it on to Ved.

I glanced at Stok, still screaming his lungs out for me, as I'd just facilitated the first reversal of the game.

I was already completely drenched in my own sweat, a sticky layer of mud, and sand.

The game moved on, passing through reversal after reversal. The other team scored first, then second, but we came back strong, scoring twice in a row ourselves. We both had strong pairs of fourths.

The other team scored their third point with twenty-two seconds left on the clock, sealing the match. The buzzer sounded and I dared a glance at Thondi, wondering if I'd disappointed him.

He put a hand on my shoulder. "You did good."

Our teams met in the center for the ritual handshaking.

A guy from the other team sneered at me though. Something in his eyes. Thoughts of seventh year rushed back to me.

"Something wrong?" I asked.

"You'll choose University," he mumbled.

"Maybe. Maybe not. What's it matter?"

Two referees' faces turned toward us.

He shifted his weight. "Nothing. Forget it."

I turned to where Stok stood. A cloud hung over him. My parents and Arnault talked idly, oblivious to the smear of doubt and fear plastered across his face. His muscles quivered as though he were moments away from jumping the fence and running to my aid.

I finished shaking hands as quickly as I could and ran to him.

Stok clasped my shoulder "What'd he say to you?" That caught my parents' attention.

"Nothing," I said. "It was nothing."

Stok's eyes took on an intensity I'd never seen before. "Le, what'd he say?"

I leaned in and whispered in his ear. "He was upset because he thought I'd choose University."

Stok's eyes grew wider. His voice dropped to a whisper. "The Holy Way's got people our age?"

My dad appeared at my side, concern etched onto his features. "Is there a problem, Le?"

"No." I shook my head. "Really, it was nothing—"

The scratchy blare of monktech horns resounded. People around us turned to one another with furrowed brows. The background chatter intensified, growing surprised and incredulous.

"It's too early," mom said.

Dad pulled up his handy. "Definitely too early."

I spotted other people checking their handies, but another blast erupted, and the crowd shuffled anxiously toward the Monastery.

"What about the last two rounds of games?" a passerby asked her colleague.

Stok and I shared a disconcerted glance.

I reached out for his hand just as he reached for mine. We held tightly the whole way to the Monastery.

The crowd grew thicker. The majority of Rig's population amassed upon the Monastery hillside.

The Reader's amplified voice became intelligible as we drew closer. He stood atop a pedestal in front of the Monastery holding a monktech cube in front of his mouth. His features lay hidden beneath his hood and robes.

His recitation boomed down the hillside. "The technologs said, 'Your ways are sick. You are a menace.' The avatars said, 'Our ways are our own. We will not threaten you. We wish to live as we are.' The technologs were more

72

powerful, and they cast the avatars out, to another world entirely. The avatars wept for losing their Divine One, just as they named their new world. They called it Alterra.

"The avatars were surprised to discover that the metaxic portal from Asura did not close behind them. 'Can we go back?' they wondered aloud. Just as some decided to risk a trip back to Asura, a message from the technologs arrived through the portal. 'Should you grow intelligent, should you come to see the true and right way of technological development, then send your Messenger back through to your true home. Should we deem him or her to represent you well, you will all be welcomed back with open arms.' And thus the portal remained."

Stok squeezed tighter.

People packed together, crowding tighter. I was almost as close to Arnault and my parents as I was to Stok.

"This year," the monk said, "there shall be a Messenger."

An angry roar went up from roughly half the crowd. Arnault and my parents stood furtively silent, but many booed loudly.

"Resist zealotry!" One woman roared.

A small contingent began chanting: "Oppression! Oppression!"

"Religious fanatics!" A man screamed.

"Our chosen Messenger—" The monk paused a beat. My heart stopped. In that moment, all the people, the sun and heat, my sweat-soaked tunic, the screaming and booing, my parents and Arnault, all of that fell away. There was just me and Stok and the Reader, concealed behind his hood, and I knew exactly what he was going to say. I mouthed the words along with him. "Is Stok Thiksay."

I turned to Stok. Stok turned to me. We looked into one another's eyes.

For one brilliant moment, I saw universes collide within those spheres. A range of emotions from fear through love through elation through heartbreak danced across his pupils.

Someone pulled him away. I was jerked backward. His hand slipped out of mine, and I screamed. Reason and logic fell away. I became a mass of muscle and flesh yelling Stok's name, but he disappeared, falling further and further away into a melee of fists and shouts, blood and violence.

"*Stok!*" I yelled again and again.

He disappeared behind a woman who kneed a man in the groin. She fell to the ground herself, pummeled by a man twice her size.

Hands grabbed me, and I tried to claw them away, but they held tight.

"It's Mom!" I heard. She pulled me away.

Dad appeared at my side, pulling me back as well.

"They've got Stok!" I yelled. "Let me go!"

They pulled me back, further and further. I struggled against them.

"They're taking Stok! *Let me go!*"

My parents pulled me, dodging fists and feet. I saw the danger everywhere, but all I could think of was Stok hurtling down a blue tunnel to a world no Alterran had ever returned from.

I struggled out of my parents' grip and surged up the hill.

Something hard contacted my head. My face hit the gritty earth, and everything went black.

I awoke in a white room, my vision blurry.

"It's okay, Honey." Mom stood to my left.

"Keep calm, Le." Dad on my right.

"What happened?" I asked, my memories a jumble.

I looked at them, though their faces remained brownish blurs atop gray clothes. I blinked and squinted. Their features seeped into focus. I think Mom was biting her lip.

"You were hit in the head, son," Dad said. "At the Festival. Do you remember?"

I took a deep breath.

"Yeah, the Festival. I was running." My memories righted themselves and history slammed into me. "Stok! Where's Stok?"

I tried to pull myself out of bed, but my vision blurred and smeared again and I fell into the sheets. Hands grasped both my arms.

"Don't strain yourself, son." Dad sounded like he was on the verge of tears.

"Honey," mom said, "you're going to be okay. You just

have to stay calm."

"*I don't want to be calm!*" I screamed and huffed. I grew dizzy. The world began spinning. Not knowing what else to do, I cried. I just bawled.

"Where's Stok?" I asked, over and over. "Where is he?"

"He's safe," Dad said.

"*Where?*" I roared, and my world spun anew.

"In the Monastery," Mom said, sobbing through her words.

I howled in rage. I screamed for Stok, for them to bring him back to me.

Doctors entered my room. They talked with Mom and Dad and I screamed for them to bring Stok back, to not let them send him away.

I felt something in my neck.

My consciousness continued screaming even after my lips stopped moving in response, and I drifted into an unwilling sleep.

I watched my feet as I trudged up the hill to the Monastery.

My handy buzzed, and I ignored it.

"Are you going to get that?" the doctor asked.

"No," I mumbled. Probably just my parents. Again. It was sweet that they cared. But the messages were getting annoying.

I looked up at the doctor, a woman in her late twenties, probably just out of University.

"How do you feel?"

Horrible.

"Fine," I said.

She gave me her best sympathetic smile. "Physically? Everything's fine?"

"Yeah. My vision is clear, and I'm not dizzy."

That shut her up. She nodded and we continued up the dusty hill in silence.

I kept my gaze on my feet, but the blue glow of the pillar of light seeped into my vision. My eyes welled up with tears.

At the entrance to the Monastery, my doctor signed the documents while I took off my shoes. I signed the documents myself without reading them.

Robed men and women took me away into the Monastery interior. The monks, normally dressed in dark crimson robes, now instead wore robes in varying shades of blue.

'Section 1: You shall be given exactly five minutes to speak with the Messenger and no more.'

The massive, empty halls felt as though they would swallow me up.

'Section 2: You shall refrain from any physical contact with the Messenger.'

They led me into a small room with only a bench in one corner and a partition in the other. I looked behind the partition. Soap and a shower head. On the bench lay a small blue piece of cloth.

"What is this? Where's Stok?"

"Did you not read the agreement?"

I closed my eyes.

'Section 3: Prior to your meeting, you must cleanse and purify yourself. You will meet him wearing only holy garments.'

"Right," I said.

"We will wait outside," the monk said. He and the others left.

I stripped off my clothes and threw them against at the foot of the partition, as there was no other furniture in the room, and I didn't want to risk them touching the blue cloth on the bench.

I stood behind the partition, scrubbing dutifully, starting, like I always did, with my neck, then my shoulders, then my arms. I made it halfway down my left arm, when despondency overtook me. My back hit the wall, and I slid to the floor. My feet slipped over the drain, the sound of water drops plunking through it, downward into some abyss, some unknown world that even water drops couldn't fathom, let alone myself.

I picked myself up and finished scrubbing.

I rinsed, turned off the water.

I found nothing to dry myself with, and so I rubbed at my hair and wicked water off my skin with my hands.

I went to the bench and picked up the blue cloth. Thin fabric of swirling blue composed it, strips less than an inch wide. Were it not for the pouch, I wouldn't have known what to do with it.

I slipped on the stretchy loincloth, did another pass at wicking water off myself with my hands, and trudged out of the room.

'*Section 4: Your conversation with the Messenger will be monitored in real time and recorded.*'

I walked down the hallway feeling exposed and alone. I just wanted to go back to the way things were before the Festival. Before there had been Resurgences and Holy Ways. Why couldn't they just leave me and Stok in peace?

'*Section 5: Should you attempt to fill the Messenger's mind with lewd, pernicious, or other thoughts deemed by the monitors to be unholy, the conversation will be aborted before the five minutes have elapsed.*'

A shiver ran through me.

We passed by the door with the ten locks and the blue glow about its edges.

I took a deep breath.

The hall we passed was lined with monks standing guard. Two of them joined up alongside my contingent, bringing my entourage to six. Really? Six burly monks against a wet, mostly naked eighteen-year-old? What did they think I was capable of?

Four guards stood outside a door. That must have been his.

I breathed in deeply, but I couldn't stop my hands from quaking. I couldn't hold back tears.

The door opened, and two monks exited the room.

I was ushered inside. The door closed with a click.

The room was white and sterile, just like the place where I'd showered. Stok had a bench and a shower, too. He sat on the bench wearing a loincloth like mine.

"Can I sit down?" I asked, feeling my face squish itself up against my will.

He nodded. My feet took me to the bench. I sat on the far side. I'd not be kicked out over the worry that I might touch him, though I desperately wanted to bring him into my arms and tell him I'd fight the entire province to be with him.

"I heard... you didn't fight them?"

Stok nodded again.

"Why...?"

"Because," his voice stuttered. Tears erupted from his eyes. "This is it, Le. What I never thought I'd be able to accomplish. Not in a million years."

"You *really* want... to go?"

"The most arrogant of the Asurans, the ones who would not cooperate, would not work to reconcile their differences with others, those were our ancestors, Le. What if me going through is what convinces them to help us—?" His head dropped.

My eyes must have been red and shot through. I glared at him. "You told me... you told me you wanted us to be together too!"

He breathed in and out, brought his hands up to his face. "I do, Le. Oh, Divine One, I really, really wish I could have both."

I gazed at him. I hadn't really believed what they'd told me. I had thought they were holding him against his will.

He continued. "Access to the portal is covered in hundreds of years of legalism and dogma. The Messenger tradition is the only thing that transcends all that, and it had been cancelled so long ago. I never imagined this was possible, Le. But now that it is..."

"Why you?"

Stok shook his head. "I don't know."

"Are they treating you okay?"

"Yeah."

"Have you seen your granddad?"

"A couple of times, yeah."

"And—?"

"He says I get to make my own decisions. I can tell he's worried about me."

Stok wiped away tears and scooted a little closer to me, keeping just enough distance. "Le, do you remember what I taught you that second night?"

"Yes, but, what does that—?"

"This is like that. I'm so, so sorry, Le. I have to do this."

Tears welled up within me anew. *"I can't go on without you!"*

"Le." Stok's face betrayed the emotional war raging within him. "You know that's not true. You can and you will. And I won't be gone long anyway."

"You don't know that!" I slammed my fists into the

bench. "There were over two hundred Messengers and *none of them ever came back!*"

"I'm sorry, Le. I've already made up my mind."

Words hurtled through my head. Hateful, vile words. I'd prepared myself for this, told myself that my last words to him couldn't be this way. I wouldn't do that to myself or to him.

Searching for something, anything I could say at all, I landed on the one truth that seemed appropriate. "I love you, Stok. I want to be with you. Please stay with me."

Stok closed his eyes for many moments, tears at the edges.

He opened them. "I love you too, Le. But I have to do this. Please be strong for me."

I reached out for him without thinking. He lurched to a stance and backed away. Monks rushed into the room and grabbed me.

"Stok!" I wailed.

"I'll come back!" Stok shouted. "I promise."

A monk pulled me by the arm and shoved me back into the room with my clothes. I changed and exited the Monastery, sobbing the whole way.

Three days later, I was lying in bed, as I'd done for the whole of those three days, ever since coming home from the Monastery.

My parents wanted me at home. Even though the doctors were still dealing with everyone from the Festival they came and saw me in my home all the same. They expected me to make a full recovery from the concussion. If I started experiencing blackouts or lost time, I was supposed to tell my parents or call them immediately.

It never happened, though I wished that it had. I wanted to lose time. I wanted to forget.

When my parents were around, I stayed in bed. When they weren't, I curled up in a ball in the corner and cried. I bawled my eyes raw.

On that third day, as I lay in bed, holding back tears so as not to worry my parents, a blue light filled my room.

I looked out the window, and saw the pillar of blue reach off the Monastery roof and into the sky, glowing so brightly. Swirling blue light rippled across sand and mud and river, over the zones, over the University, over all of Rig.

It flashed and was gone.

He was gone.

I hid in my pillows, and I bawled fresh tears.

"Divine One save us," I said.

"Divine One have mercy upon our souls," the monk said.

She held a computer pad before me with a document on its screen. I pressed my thumb into the computer. I'd read this one a billion times already.

"When do I begin?" I asked.

"Right now," the monk said.

"How many others are there?"

"None."

"I'm the only one at remedial level?"

A nod.

"Are you my teacher?"

"I am."

"What may I call you, master?"

"Master Nurla will do."

"Thank you, Master Nurla."

"You may change in here."

I entered the white room with the solitary bench and shower. I fought back a wave of grief at the unwanted memories, and collected myself. I changed into the maroon robes that waited for me on the bench.

With a few deep, steadying breaths, I exited back into the hallway. "What should I do with my old clothes, Master Nurla?"

"They will be taken care of. Do you know of the Ancillary Outer Chamber?"

I shook my head.

"Every day your clothes will be stored there in a special locker just for you. I will show you after today's lessons. I need to ask you something, Novice Le."

"Yes, Master?"

We stopped walking. She turned to me and pulled down her hood. She had long, dark hair and deep black skin. She wore glasses and had bright, intelligent eyes.

"Why did you decide to enter the Monastery at the remedial level?"

"Messenger Stok was—"

"Is," she corrected.

I gulped. "Messenger Stok taught me that the Monastery has value. Though I chose my courses as though for University, I want to honor his— his existence in Asura by discovering what it was about Monastery that drew him here."

Master Nurla eyed me warily. She pulled her hood up and began down the hall once more.

"Are you ready for your first lesson, Novice Le?"

"I am."

COMMUNITY

[Stok]

The blue rippled around me, a sea of dye, pulling, turning, twisting, seething. Cyan and navy and beryl morphed and swirled around me. I stood and gazed, awestruck. If any experience could come close to witnessing the Divine One, this would be it.

I reached out to touch the colors, which appeared to lie mere meters from me. I stepped forward and tripped, falling forward. I reached out, and my hands contacted an invisible, curved barrier. I gazed down beyond them into the blue.

The azure torrents shimmered and congealed.

They turned maroon.

My barrier flashed and I fell. My hand crashed into metallic shards of grass, and I cried out in pain.

I scrambled to a stance and looked down at my bloody hands. Silver dripped from the wounds. I tore my eyes away and looked around myself.

Dry, brownish-black hills rolled away toward the horizon, all of them patched with clumps of metallic grass, like the one I'd landed in. The sky was a deep maroon, though the sun was high. The sun, at least, appeared normal.

Not what I'd expected of Asura at all. History told of a blue sky and green, fertile meadows. Trees with bright green foliage, wheat and flowers. Paradise.

The ground rumbled. A hill in the distance ruptured like a burst bubble and flattened of its own accord. Its patches of grass disintegrated.

Fear struck me. I looked down at my hand and screamed. Lines of metal traced their way along my right hand like veins, covering my skin. They encased my fingers and began trailing up my forearm.

Not knowing what else to do, I took off running.

Sweat dripped down my face.

My neck itched, then tingled, then burned. I ripped at my collar and felt my neck with my good hand. Metallic.

"Someone help me!" I screamed. Oh, Asura. I had given up Le and Arnault and a joyful, prosperous life for this? Had the Asurans of four centuries ago really been so hateful and callous as to send a false message, to give us a portal to hell, all the while telling us it was the path to salvation?

No. If they'd wanted our ancestors dead, they would have killed them. It made no sense.

"*Inferus!*" The voice erupted from behind me, metallic and monotone.

I ran faster, but was grabbed and hauled into the air.

A beast appeared before me, like a man, but twice as tall. He was lanky and his whole body shimmered steel gray. His eyes glowed orange, and holograms projected off his naked, metallic body. His legs were haunched back like a quadruped's, but he stood upright. His hands and feet were elongated. Sinuous fingers wrapped around my entire body and squeezed.

The thing snarled, revealing a row of sharp, silver teeth. *"You are from the portal. You have defenses. How? The homo sapiens inferus of Altnaraka forsook progress."*

"Who are you—?" I screamed, and my voice turned clanky, like metal scraping across metal. Pain shot through my throat.

"You will be improved." The creature grinned and its eyes flared.

Gunshots. The creature howled.

I tumbled to the ground. My vision blurred.

"Anti-nanogenics!" A woman's voice. She sounded human.

Other voices. Men and women both. They sounded human too.

My blurred vision turned black.

"I'm blind!" I yelled, my voice a metallic monotone.

"I'm going to give you a sedative." The woman's voice. A hand, presumably hers, gripped my bicep. "You'll be alright. We've got him!"

My chest burned and my entire torso itched.

"Le..." I mumbled. "I'm so sorry. I was wrong."

I let the calm of sleep take me away.

[Shey]

...And so, the benevolence of the Divine One appears uncertain. He says he will grant salvation only to those who follow all his 'holy' prescriptions, and the rest of us are doomed to eternal damnation. It appears, in this, he is nothing more than a snake oil salesman who uses the fear of the unknown to prevent the spread of ideas that contradict his existence.

The only possible purpose that an all-powerful Divine One could have to present such fear tactics is control, and that would make him, by definition, less than divine. He is a contradiction in terms. He cannot exist.

In reality, he is merely a boogieman invoked by a governmental body in order to control a population too superstitious and ignorant to embrace the only things that have ever mattered for human development: science and technology.

I stopped and read the words out loud again. I smiled to myself. Especially the flourish at the end. Great stuff.

I took a deep breath.

Maybe one more read through? No, Shey. No. Just send it. You've worked on this enough.

I read it through once more all the same. I desperately wanted this one to be selected for the Resurgence Bulletin. It was far and away my best essay yet.

I opened up a new mail dialog and pulled the file into it.

Another deep breath.

Shey, you can do this.

I stared at the send button, my fingers unmoving.

I closed my eyes and conjured my most positive thoughts.

Your spelling and grammar were superb. Your logic was impeccable, as always. They'll take it. They have to. Please, let them take it.

I opened my eyes.

Second opinion. I needed a second opinion.

My countenance fell. I sat and stared at my handy.

A memory shot through mind like an exploding firecracker.

Taro. Lunch.

I looked at the clock on my screen.

Twelve thirty. Damn it!

I grabbed up my computer and rushed out the door. I hurtled through streets and busy thoroughfares. All my classes and research, I could keep it all straight in my head. I could manage complex equations and computer software architecture while crafting beautiful prose about cultural advancement. And yet I couldn't remember jack when it came to Taro.

I walked in the door to the restaurant panting and sweaty.

Taro sat, a plate of pasta and his computer before him.

I sat down across from him.

"Hi," I said.

He looked up from his research. "Hi."

"Sorry I'm late."

"Not a problem."

"I was working on that essay for the Resurgence Bulletin."

Taro took a sip of his drink. "I was just catching up on software design theory."

I blinked. Taro always did this. He didn't get mad. I'd almost prefer if he did. It was almost like... he didn't care.

"Are you angry?" I asked.

Taro shook his head.

"Did you read my essay?" I tried.

"Yeah. It was good." He took another bite of pasta. "I liked it."

I came close to letting out a long, exasperated sigh. The first few times Taro had done this, it had been cute and endearing. I'd thrown a small party in my mind, sticking my tongue out at a one-year-younger Le, who had cast critical doubt on all my arguments, who had questioned my every assumption, who had attempted to undermine every bit of my logic, no matter how impeccable or factually-backed.

And here sat Taro, the unending mantra. 'It was good.' 'I liked it.'

I should like Taro better. I should prefer this. All of Le's incessant nagging, his belittlement of all the hard work the Resurgence did to *make his world better*. And he'd thrown it all away for that lunatic,

I'd heard Stok had been sneaking into zones, which is probably what had led Le there. A damned incubus, that bastard. The Messenger tradition was too good for him. They should have locked him up in quarantine instead.

"You want to go to the library with me later?" Taro asked.

Not really.

"Sure," I said. "See you there after class."

I stood up.

"You're not going to eat?" Taro asked.

"I'd just keep you late, and I'm not very hungry. I won't miss lunch next time, I promise. Tomorrow's on me, okay?"

Taro smiled happily and wiped sauce off his face with his napkin.

I exited the restaurant as quickly as I could.

When I reached the walls of Zone B, I turned left. I wasn't sure why I turned left. My legs just took me that way.

The throngs dispersed as I wound my way around the edge of the zone and out into the sand between the University and the Monastery, the ground reserved for the Festival. The events of last year hadn't even put a dent in this year's schedule–preparations for this year's Festival were already underway. Metal poles sat tied up in bunches. Boxes of streamers held layers of paper in this year's colors: maroon and yellow-orange. Some of the grounds were already set up for sports.

I spotted the voidball court, the square of squares etched into the ground. The void generator sat at the center. I recalled Le. I remembered watching him, thinking how wonderfully he complimented his counterpart third-quarterman in the game. That hulking mass was all the skill and strength and speed, but Le was the finesse. Graceful and strong in his own way.

I'd spotted Le about town. He wore the crimson robes of a novice everywhere, even though most novices wore their casual clothes outside the Monastery. A cloud hung over his head, and I never saw him with anyone else, except his parents once.

The voidball game was the last time I'd seen him happy. It was the last time I'd seen Stok. Messenger Stok, one year gone, and not so much as a peep from the portal. Unsurprising. Who would give this place a second thought upon arriving on a world with centuries of technological advancement on us and enormous human and material resources at its disposal? No matter how naive a person is about religion, comfort is comfort. It should surprise no one that they all stay.

Even as such thoughts drifted through my mind, I found myself heading down the solitary Monastery road, the one that weaved through the Festival grounds, now more of a construction site.

I climbed the hill, counting each of the one hundred seventy-two steps.

The monks at the gate stepped forward. You may not

enter."

"I thought this was free hour?" I asked.

The one monk turned to the other. "The sun looks low in the sky, doesn't it?"

"Yes," the other monk said. "Very low. I think free hour has passed."

I pulled up my computer and showed them the screen. "It's only twelve forty-three."

The first monk smiled condescendingly. "I'm sorry, your logical eminence, but we feeble-minded, ignorant religious types don't understand complex computery things. I'm afraid I can't read your fancy, University-issued computer."

I huffed. "Can you just get Le to come out here then?"

The second monk rolled her eyes. "I'll summon him with my inferior religious technology. It may take some time."

I did my best to keep my tone level. "Thank you."

I tapped my foot. What was I doing here? Le had made it clear he never wanted to see me again. I was wasting my time and his.

"Shey?"

I turned. "Le!"

The guards eyed Le and me warily.

"It's okay," Le said. They returned to their posts.

"Kinda sensitive, aren't they?"

"You telling me the University is less sensitive?"

"Point taken."

Le raised an eyebrow at me.

"What?"

Le shook his head. "Nothing."

We stood in silence.

"So—" We both began at the same time.

"You go," he said.

"Le... I need your help with something."

"I'm busy."

"Please."

He sighed and rolled his shoulders. "I can't believe I'm... what is it?"

"An essay. I want you... to tell me what's wrong with it."

Le stared at me like I had grown a second head. "What?"

"It's already been rejected three times, so there must be something wrong with it and I don't know what it is and it needs to be perfect."

"Just a sec." Le pulled a monktech cube from his pocket and pressed a button on its surface. "Can you say that last part again?"

I furrowed my brow. "Is that a recording device?"

"Say that last part again. About *needing my help* to make something *perfect*."

I threw up my arms. "Fine, Le. Be this way."

I turned and marched down the hill.

"I'll do it," Le called out from behind me.

I stopped and turned. He smiled, but his eyes were sad.

Sad beyond belief. The fact that such sadness could not override a joke at my expense should have told me something.

"Thank you, Le."

"You're welcome. Say hi to Taro for me."

I walked back down the hill and mailed him the file. I'd be late to fifth period for sure.

My memories following my blindness were rapt and contorted, as though I drifted seamlessly between dream and reality.

I think at one point I awoke, and my vision had returned. I lay on a mattress in some kind of chamber with red metal walls. Holographic computer screens lined the room. Men and women with light skin and yellow hair lay in beds around me. Some slept, others moaned. I held up my right hand and a metal claw came into view instead. I stretched my silver pincer fingers and then I screamed.

I had other visions too. A woman, yellow hair and blue eyes, a kind face. She came to me and asked me questions. I think I provided intelligible answers, but she always seemed confused, like I was mad, though I felt perfectly sane.

All at once, I sat up in my bed.

I wiped sweat from my brow, wriggling my fingers. Both sets appeared human. I rubbed at my arms and neck, happy to feel no traces of metal.

The people I remembered from my liminal state were

still here. Most had large, metallic feet and huge legs, engorged from their thighs down. Some of the men had the metal streaked across their chest, shoulders and arms, all enormous and out of proportion. Such individuals wore no shirts. I stood up and walked slowly around. Some of them had glowing, holographic eyes, too, some kind of ocular implant.

The woman from my dreams appeared in the doorway, the one with yellow hair and blue eyes. She smiled when she saw me. She possessed the enlarged legs and feet.

"Hi," I muttered.

A man directly to my right groaned loudly. I knelt down and looked him over. His eyes remained closed. His head jerked left and right.

"Is there anything to do for him?" I asked.

"No," the woman said. "Not that we haven't already done. It's up to him now. His name is Tarangar. Because of you, he might live. Normally, his exposure would have been lethal."

I backed away from him. "Exposure to what?"

"The evolvers."

I bit my lip.

She nodded weakly. "You have a lot of catching up to do. Follow me."

She led me out of the room and down a poorly lit corridor of crimson metal walls. About half the lights in the ceiling were dysfunctional. A few spat sparks

"My name's Stok."

She cast me a wan smile. "You told me already."

I frowned. "I don't remember that."

"That's to be expected. Now, if you keep losing memories, then we'll have a problem, but I suspect you'll be fine."

"What's your name?"

"Kish."

"Did you save my life?"

"Yes."

"Thank you."

"No need. You've done more for us than you can imagine."

"Is that what you were talking about earlier? How that man may live because of me?"

She nodded. "We assumed the avatars had destroyed the nanites that made the journey with them. It seems we were wrong."

I blinked a few times. "I had nanites in me? From Alterra?"

"You didn't know?"

I shook my head. Thoughts coalesced and snapped into place. Of course! Le's experiment to test the zones. The nanites must have interacted with my DNA in the petri dish, then hitched a ride out of the zones inside of me.

I broke a grin. "But I think I know how it happened."

We turned a corner and walked into an expansive, busy room, covered with computer equipment. A holographic map on the back wall displayed a portion of land, roughly a circle, with an ever-shifting border. The red line denoting the perimeter wobbled chaotically.

People walked about, many with shoeless metallic feet and engorged legs, handing each other computers, tapping buttons, and talking.

Another class of people sat motionless at their computer consoles, unspeaking and unmoving. Windows appeared and disappeared before them at lightning speed, far too fast for me to read their contents.

I approached one of the sitting people and looked into his eyes. He had no pupils, and his eyeballs jittered madly in their sockets. More than a dozen such individuals sat at similar computer stations.

I turned to Kish. "What are they doing?"

"Keeping the deranged and their evolvers out of our compound."

"Do they take shifts?"

Kish shook her head, pain evident on her face.

"The deranged think thousands of times faster than we do. These brave individuals work nonstop. They have given up their human minds so that the rest of us may keep ours."

Orange lighting flared from holographic monitors and sirens erupted.

"Perimeter breach." The voice was cold and mechanical, erupting over the speakers.

"Stay here." Kish shot out the door, her huge legs taking her away in loping strides. Others followed her. Mere seconds later, the room's only occupants were me and the motionless individuals with wobbling eyes.

I scowled and ran out the door.

I turned corner after corner of neglected, crimson metal hallways, following the sound of their voices and the clangs of their feet against the floor grating. I ran up a flight of stairs and came out onto a plain of brown dirt. Glass structures housing green plants dotted the landscape. I spotted a well to my right. Orange light erupted intermittently from points in space throughout the sky, accompanying the siren.

Thanks to the transparency of the structures, I was able to spot Kish and her contingent. I broke into a sprint, hurtling around the greenhouses toward their position.

I turned a corner beyond the fourth greenhouse and screeched to a halt. Kish and seven others stood before a shimmering, wobbling red wall of static haze that stretched up into the sky. Indeed, the faint red haze wobbled above my head as well, perhaps ten or twelve meters up–a dome.

Kish and the others tapped at panels that projected from their arms. One woman with an ocular implant projected her computer from her eye.

The red haze blobbed inward, gaining ground, a bulbous protrusion, eating up our safe zone. The group tapped faster.

Suddenly, the orange lights ceased. The sirens went off.

The group breathed a sigh of relief. The protrusion

halted its advance, but remained. The majority of the entourage walked away, frowning and eyeing me as they passed.

Kish stopped in front of me. "I told you to stay inside. These events can be dangerous."

I crossed my arms. "Is this really Asura?"

"Come with me back into the compound," Kish said. "And I'll answer all your questions."

I walked into the arboretum, and the entire complex went silent. Everyone stared at me except for Taro, who looked away.

I tilted my head, perplexed. I walked through the awkward sea of eyes toward Taro.

I approached him and reached out for his arm. "Taro, what's—?"

He walked away.

Just slunk into the crowd like a sand vole.

I gaped, befuddled.

"Candidate Shey," a female voice said. I turned toward it. Hajli, a tall woman with an imposing gaze–somewhere high up in the Resurgence hierarchy, I couldn't remember her station exactly–stood beside me.

I worked to get my mouth moving again. "Yes, Master Hajli?"

"Come with me."

Conversation within the arboretum resumed. Her heels clicked as we walked outside into the sea of still grass.

The whistling wind and chatter of the Resurgence gathering both whispered in the background.

At five meters from the door, Hajli turned on her heeled shoes and looked down at me. "I understand you paid a visit to the Monastery today."

I crossed my arms. "So what if I did? That's not illegal."

"It's not." She bunched up her lips. "But someone in your position needs to show more discretion."

"I didn't know the Resurgence was picking my friends for me."

"We are your friends. If we're not, we can always arrange a less vital role for you within the organization."

I narrowed my eyes. "What's this *really* about?"

She eyed me like a saber snake. "Tell me about your business at the Monastery today, and I will answer your question."

I returned her gaze. "I asked an old friend for some editing help. That's all."

"There are many talented editors within the University."

I chortled.

Hajli leveled her gaze. "You disagree?"

I threw out my arms. "Everyone I've shown my essays to at the University—professors, other candidates, dozens of people—they've all said my logic is impeccable, my structure is sound. It's almost like..."

Hajli quirked her lips ever so slightly. A thought

worked its way through my mind. I'd had it before, and I'd shot it down in the past. It was too ridiculous. Too unfathomable. But now, in the face of Hajli's superior smile...

Against all Logic, I gave voice to my thoughts. "It's almost like the Resurgence won't publish *anything* I write, regardless of quality. As though the problem isn't the content or the structure of the writing, but its author."

Hajli's superior smile faded into a morose calm. Her muscles tensed.

Vile emotions churned within me. I bit my tongue, but held her gaze firm.

"Your former boyfriend," Hajli spoke the syllables with intense precision, "was it him you went to see today?"

"He's one of the smartest people I know and should *be* at the University!" I spat back. "He doesn't belong in that place!"

Hajli smiled sardonically, the smile of a sand weevil that had just skewered its prey. "Yes, of course. *Novice* Le."

I could see her gears turning. She was imagining holding onto this information, using it to leverage favors out of me lest she tell Taro I was paying visits to my ex. The joke was on her. After tonight's performance, I doubted there was a 'Shey and Taro' to salvage.

"I can't believe you've done this to me. After all my effort, all my hard work for the organization—"

Hajli stopped me with a raise of her eyebrows. "The Holy Way is arranging for another Messenger this year."

"*What?!*"

"Keep your voice down!"

I huffed and panted. "They can't be that stupid. Don't they realize they got lucky? The only reason they got away with it last year was because that idiot Stok *wanted* to go."

"They will choose someone else stupid and deluded. We are talking about the Monastery, after all. They fall on their swords for even the flimsiest of rationales. The Divine One need only speak through their 'righteous' leaders, and they can be convinced of anything. They're not like us, Shey. You can't try to understand them based on how you'd react. You have logic and reason. They don't."

Such words had always reassured me in the past, made me feel righter. Better. But this was Le. He had logic and reason. I knew he did. Was it grief that had driven him to make the choice that would leave his adult life in ruins? Could he be so sad he'd destroy himself? Or had there been more to his decision than I'd given him credit for?

Hajli interrupted my thoughts. "You must see this from our point of view. The Holy Way is strengthening its position within Parliament. Lines are being drawn. And two years ago, you brought us Le. He was argumentative, condescending, aloof, and *then*—"

I waved my hands in exasperation. "He changed his affiliation at the last minute."

"And now *you're* sneaking off to see him. It makes us wonder..."

I scoffed and shook my head back and forth. "Deciding who I can talk to in my free time...?"

Hajli twisted up her lips and glowered. "Speak with Novice Le again, and I will move for your expulsion from the Resurgence."

"You *can't*—"

Her eyes became daggers, her voice venom. "Not a word."

I tapped my foot and considered my next move carefully. "Fine."

Hajli smiled. "I'm glad we understand each other. Now, I was hoping you could come tell Nabha about your ideas for science events during the Festival."

She turned but I remained, momentarily staring out into the still grass, listening to it whisper in the breeze.

"Candidate Shey?"

"Yes," I said. "I'm coming."

I followed her back into the arboretum.

I followed in Kish's wake as we returned underground to the control room. She told me to stay put by the door and busied herself talking to others. I leaned against the doorframe and stared at the ceiling.

It seemed unreal. How could this be Asura? Everyone on Alterra knew our history. The avatars had been kicked off Asura and sent to a parallel universe. I'd always assumed that had happened because us Alterrans were stubborn and mentally inflexible. It fit with my view of my society.

In my mind, I'd painted a picture of the Asurans as

both technologically and spiritually advanced. I'd convinced myself that the configuration of this society could heal the self-destructive path my own faced.

So much for that.

And now I'd lost Le and Arnault.

Divine One, what have I done?

"Come with me." Kish walked out the door beside me. I followed.

We walked down just one hallway, turned a corner and entered another room, this one much smaller. A desk sat in the center, and a light flickered overhead. Kish picked up a computer pad, the smallest one I had ever seen, and tapped a few buttons. She grunted and jumped up onto her desk in a single leap. She pulled a panel from the ceiling and fiddled with the technological guts of the light.

"This is really Asura?" I asked. "Four hundred years ago there were avatars and technologs, and the technologs banished the avatars to a parallel universe?"

"That's right." The light stabilized and Kish jumped down. Her metallic feet left a slight indentation in the floor. "I propose a trade. The last four hundred years of Asuran history for the last four hundred years of... Alterran history. Interesting choice of name, by the way." Kish sat down at her desk, and motioned for me to have a seat as well.

I pulled a rusty chair out of the corner. "You don't know our history? What happened to all the other Messengers?"

"The deranged and their evolvers got to them first. You were very lucky. We happened to be in the area, and the nanites you brought with you slowed the transformation long enough for us to get to you."

A sickening feeling worked its way up from my stomach. I put my hand over my mouth.

Kish eyed me. "You okay?"

I nodded and breathed deeply. The nausea passed. "I'll be fine."

"You first," Kish said.

"Like I said, my ancestors, the avatars, arrived on Alterra four hundred years ago. And they got your message about sending people back so that we could rejoin your society. We established our Monastery on the hill with the metaxic portal.

"After a few generations, a population of technological adepts emerged, and as they grew up, they banded together and formed the University.

"The two institutions became the center of our culture. We organized a government, even divided Parliament along those lines. The House of Analytics sides with the University and the House of Souls with the Monastery.

"I read that the two worked together pretty well at first, but in my lifetime, they've been nothing but hostile toward one another. When I was chosen as Messenger, I watched my whole city beat and attack one another over whether or not I should be allowed to—"

I choked on my own words

"I'm sorry." I shook my head. "That's nothing compared to the suffering here."

Kish raised a hand. "It's all right. A society fighting over its ideas... Asurans understand that implicitly."

I tilted my head.

"What you see all around you, what little remains of Resistance Cell A5, are the meager faithful of Asura."

"Meager faithful?"

Kish nodded. "Five hundred years ago, the last two remaining global superpowers decided to join hands in harmony and create the country of Veda. With the collaboration of all world powers and a global agreement that technological progress would be mankind's highest priority, the stage appeared set for a bright and prosperous future.

"There was just one problem. On this continent, there existed a province of people who did not embrace technological progress the same way that the newly organized Veda government did. Over the course of the first one hundred years of the Veda government, the 'avatars' sank further and further into disfavor with the mainstream culture for refusing to immediately embrace and incorporate new technologies into their lives.

"Four hundred years ago, citing 'extreme backwardness' and 'toxic, zealatrous ideology,' your people were cast out to Alterra using the newly discovered metaxic transfer technology. Us Asurans became free to pursue technological advancement unimpeded by 'petty, ignorant and superstitious concerns' about the sanctity of human life, and the ethics of purity.

"At first, things were grand. We cured genetic diseases, diminished the adverse effects of aging, improved physical agility and motor coordination, visual acuity, even accelerated the potential of the human brain.

"However, when some scientists suggested completely rewriting the DNA for eyes, ears, noses, hearts, and even brains to make them 'better,' they met no resistance. When they suggested that any IQ below 450 was 'unacceptable,' they met no resistance. When they started rewriting the human genome, fundamentally changing human speech, analytical thought, emotion and perception, they met no resistance. The Vedans kept making themselves 'better' until they became unrecognizable as anything remotely human. They became the deranged. And they're still at it, 'improving themselves' endlessly.

"Three hundred twenty years ago the ruling council of the government called Veda ceased to exist in any meaningful sense. The deranged, former humans, wander Asura, reshaping it at will to make it more 'perfect.' They hunt us as though we're animals."

"Divine One save us," I muttered.

Kish's voiced became hushed. "We speak that same prayer every day before bed and upon waking."

I gulped. "Not to diminish what you've done for me... but can we go back to the portal? There are people on Alterra I care about. And if I can tell them about your situation, then maybe—"

Kish shook her head back and forth.

"Our ancestors hid our side of the portal from the deranged with some kind of quantum distortion technology three hundred years ago, right before their outpost was overrun. No one understood the technology except them. We can get you back to where we found you, but we don't have a way to open the portal before the deranged overrun us."

The door to Kish's office burst open. A man appeared. "A2's power plant is about to go."

"Shit!" Kish slammed a fist on the table. "Get the contingent together."

She sprang up from her seat with lightning agility.

"Wait!" I shouted. "I want to help."

Kish shook her head. "You'll need enhanced legs where we're going. And nanogenic inoculations."

"You can undo the leg enhancements, like you did my arm, right?"

Kish nodded to the man, and he ran off down the hall. She turned back to me. "Yes."

"Then inoculate me. Give me the enhancements."

She locked her eyes onto me for a mere second. "Go to the medical bay." And she loped off.

Unease and uncertainty, despair and regret surged through me. I trudged to the medical bay.

I was about to lose my human legs.

If only I'd stayed with Le.

—

Keep it calm. Keep it calm.

I felt like a lone guy on a sandy hillside, his back braced against an avalanche of sand. But I was going to make it. If I could just get inside my house and to my room, I'd be fine.

My handy beeped.

Muscle memory brought the interface to my attention before reason had a chance to override the gesture.

TARO SAID:
We still on for lunch tomorrow?

The holographic buttons were lucky they were immaterial, or my fingers would have smashed them to bits.

YOU SAID:
Go fuck yourself.

TARO SAID:
Talk to me when you're done with your tantrum.

YOU SAID:
FUCK YOU

I turned the handy off. I felt my hand throw the door open before I could stop myself, and it slammed with a deafening crash.

Logic damn it all—

"Shey!" I heard the telltale shuffling of Dad leaving the

living room. I hurried for the stairs.

Too late. Dad appeared at the base of the stairwell.

"Shey! Stop right there!"

"Please Dad, not now—"

"What are you doing, Shey?"

"I'm going to my room. To do my homework."

"Director Hajli texted me. She's worried about you."

"She's *worried* about me? Dad, that woman is twisted. These people who've floated to the top of the Resurgence this last year..."

Dad scowled. "Watch where you tread, Shey. I didn't raise you to be a religious nutter."

I scoffed and threw up my arms. "Wait, so being anti-religion means loving every member of the Resurgence now?"

"I don't know if you've noticed, Shey, but people have been *taking sides*. If you're not on our side, then you're on theirs, and theirs is the path to disease, to ignorance, to everything that's wrong with the world. They've been holding back human potential for the entirety of history, and no son of mine is taking their side. Tomorrow morning we're going to talk about what kind of apology you'll be mailing to Director Hajli."

Fuck you, Dad.

I bit my tongue and tasted blood.

I marched upstairs.

"Good night, Shey."

It was all I could do not to slam the door to my room.

Somehow, at least, I managed that.

I sat on a medical table in my underwear while Kish tapped at her computer, and I watched as metal veins spread out from my kneecaps and coursed up my legs. I felt myself grow lightheaded, watching the metal consume my legs, and had to look away, but the room started to spin and my heart felt like it would burst out of my chest.

Kish squeezed my shoulder. "Look at me."

I looked up at her, her face hard, only the faintest traces of remorse. "Where we are going, you will need to run fast. If you see a deranged, you shout, and we all run the other direction. Understand?"

I nodded.

It's hard to describe how the change in my legs felt. It didn't hurt like when the evolvers had infected me. A warm sensation coursed from my thighs down to my toes. My muscles tensed and relaxed, expanding with each contraction. My skin took on a silver sheen, my feet grew larger, and my toes curled outward into shiny claws.

"Won't I have to get used to walking again?"

Kish shook her head. "The nanite programs take care of that too."

She grabbed behind her, then shoved a pair of pants into my chest. The legs and waist would have been three sizes too big for me just a minute ago. I grabbed them up.

Kish turned around, still working at her computer. I swung myself off the table and stood, surprised at the ease of movement despite the massive changes to my physiognomy. I pulled one leg of the pants on and my foot hit the medical table and sent it flying into the next, which was, thankfully, unoccupied.

"Be careful!" Kish shot around and glared at me.

"Sorry." I finished dressing.

"You'll have to be even more careful once we leave the compound."

The man who'd interrupted our meeting entered the medical room. I saw him more clearly now. His feet were silver claws as well, but his upper body was normal. He was stocky, and long, curly, brown locks fell from his head.

"Matho, this is Stok. He's coming with us."

Matho's eyes oozed concern and skepticism. He clenched his mouth shut and eyed me warily.

"Are we ready to go?" Kish asked.

"Yes," Matho said. "Twenty-two minutes until they lose containment and abandon the reactor."

"And we're giving them three?"

Matho nodded dejectedly.

"Divine One save us."

"Three what?" I dared.

They both shot me a hard look. I held up my hands. "Hey, sorry I asked."

"No," Kish said. "If you're going to help us, you should know. We're giving them three computerminds, the people who've had their brains altered to accelerate neural processing at the expense of conscious thought."

I bit my lip, and I nodded weakly.

"We can debate the ethical quandary later," Matho said.

"I agree," Kish said. "Are you coming, Stok?"

I nodded weakly again and took off after them through the halls. None of my time in track and field could compare to the exhilaration of running like this. My legs took me down the halls at the speed of a car. I found I could dodge oncoming human traffic with incredible ease.

I followed in Kish and Matho's wake. We ran up the staircase and outside, where the same contingent who had sealed the perimeter stood huddled together.

Three of the men were shirtless, their chests, arms and backs shining silver, their muscles huge and bulging. Each held the limp body of a person with no pupils, their expressions stuck blank and mouths agape.

A holographic map appeared overtop of my vision.

"Is everyone clear on the route?" Matho shouted.

"Yes, sir!" Everyone but me replied.

"Yes, sir," I added belatedly, prompting a number of antagonistic stares from other members of the contingent.

What I wouldn't give to be at home right now packing for my expedition up the river or lying in bed with Le on freedays until eight in the morning. I'd been wrong thinking it benevolent or righteous to try to change my society for the better. It had been stupid. The right path had clearly been Le. And it would have been so easy! I would have lived and loved comfortably

Here I stood now, a stranger in a hostile, dangerous world, my genetic code altered, my body infused with machines, with no hope of ever seeing my family again. And these people–better to remain useful to them, or Divine One knew what might happen to me. They could decide I'd be more useful to them as a computermind.

Kish, Matho, and the rest of their party took off, and I ran after them.

We zoomed through the shimmering, red haze and out into the land I recognized—red sky, brown, dry hills covered in patches of metallic grass.

I drew my attention to the holographic map, which displayed the surrounding topography. At the center lay a cluster of blue dots. One of them blinked, presumably me.

A line stretched out from our group, forward through the hills. My dot remained fixed at the center, and the map moved beneath it as I ran.

Our group zoomed around some hills and over others. We came to a dried up riverbed and followed its edge for some time before crossing.

We must have been going thirty or forty kilometers per hour, and I didn't even break a sweat.

I strode up alongside Kish. "Is this our top speed?"

"No. Top speed varies by person. A lot depends on individual biology."

"Then this is a speed that everyone can go?"

"Yes."

"What's the fastest a person has ever gone?"

She shot me a dangerous look. "Why do you want to know?"

"I— uh..."

"You're enjoying this?" Her tone was accusatory.

I didn't know what to say.

"We do this to ourselves because we have to. We give up these small bits of our humanity to keep humanity as a whole alive. Remember that though this small step is relatively harmless, these abilities are not without their dangers or their scars."

I balked. "You said you could undo this!"

"That is true. But with each change comes risks. The organism as a whole is traumatized with each change. With numerous changes, there come undesirable side effects, often diseases."

I gulped and shuddered, wondering if Asura could get any worse.

When the negative thoughts had nearly crowded out all others, I turned my attention back to our flight. Huge hills appeared in the distance. My map showed us going over them.

I fell back and found myself pondering Kish's words. No good deed truly went unpunished, it seemed.

As the gradient of the ground increased, I began to notice my first signs of physical exertion. I started sweating and my heart rate quickened.

Green dots appeared on the interface, scattered across the plains beyond the hills. Our path on the map jumped about wildly, as though the computer couldn't decide where to take us. Our group slowed and came to a halt.

Kish and Matho turned their backs to the group and consulted with one another quietly. Everyone else huddled a few meters away.

A man with an enhanced upper body and a computer-mind slung over his shoulders stood at the very edge of the group. I approached him.

"Are those green dots—?"

"They're deranged." The man did even bother trying to hide his exasperation at the question, and receded into the huddled contingent. He and his friends eyed me with disdain.

I sat down on the ground, wrapped my arms around my head, and closed my eyes.

TENTH MONTH, SECOND DAY, 04:32 AM
TO: «Shey Choglamsar»
FROM: «Le Namgyal»
SUBJECT: Your Polemical Diatribe
BODY: Hi Shey,

So, Master Nurla caught me working on this and read it herself. I don't think she's ever looked at me that way before. I got my cleaning duties re-assigned to the lavatories for the next three weeks, so thanks for that.

On the plus side, Master Nurla completely scrapped her lessons for yesterday and we talked about narrative composition the whole day instead. I actually got a lot out of it. Ludhiana and Ropar were the most interesting of the bunch. Ludhiana in particular talked about optimal narrative structure and mythological archetypes. Great stuff!

It helped so much that I went through your essay a second time. You can see my comments and suggested edits.

I know you hate religion and religious people, and I'm not going to bother trying to change your mind, but I hope the irony of me helping you with your essay out of the goodness of my heart, given *my* affiliations, is not lost on you.

All the best,
Le

Tenth Month, Second Day, 07:21 AM
To: «Le Namgyal»
From: «Shey Choglamsar»
Subject: RE: Your Polemical Diatribe
Body: My Logic, Le, what time do you wake up?

Your comments look great. I like your notes on narrative structure. I'll have to look up Ludhiana. I've never heard of her(?).

And no, the irony is not lost on me.

[[I noticed that you didn't comment on the content. I was actually kind of hoping you would. Could we meet somewhere and talk more about it?]]

- Shey

Tenth Month, Second Day, 7:30 AM
To: «Shey Choglamsar»
From: «Le Namgyal»
Subject: RE: Your Polemical Diatribe
Body: I wake up at four. It's pretty common in the Monastery. You ever hear yelling over from the Monastery hill from five to seven? That's morning exercise. Two hours right as the sun comes up. I hated it at first, but now I don't know what I'd do without it.

I'm glad you found my comments useful.

[[And damn. Long time since I've seen this code. It's been what, three years since we used this script? Remember when you wrote me a lewd letter in chemistry and the teacher found it and made you read it in front of the class? I nearly died laughing. "Asterisk, asterisk, circle with a line through it, human ear, middle finger."

Anyway, why are we using code? I take it you want to meet somewhere discreet? Is there something I should know? And more importantly, is there something Taro should know?]]

Tenth Month, Second Day, 7:39 AM
To: «Le Namgyal»
From: «Shey Choglamsar»
Subject: RE: Your Polemical Diatribe
Body: [[No, this has nothing to do with Taro, or anything like that. In fact, I'll be breaking up with him today if he hasn't caught on himself that we're broken up already.

Something happened last night... I'm not even going to risk talking about it in code.

I'm being watched. I don't think anything is completely safe, not even this. As long as things don't get too bad, I don't think they'll bother translating these messages, but I'm taking a chance just reaching out to you.

Anyway, yes, you're right. I want to talk somewhere private.

I still can't believe I'm going to write this, but I was hoping you could take me into whatever zone you and Stok went to.

I know I'm asking a lot of you, Le. I know how much he meant to you. I don't want to defile his memory or anything like that.

It's honestly the only place I can think of that will be safe from the prying eyes of my 'affiliates,' other than leaving town completely, which would be incredibly suspicious in and of itself.

Le... I don't know who else to turn to. Please help.]]

Tenth Month, Second Day, 5:24 PM
To: «Shey Choglamsar»
From: «Le Namgyal»
Subject: RE: Your Polemical Diatribe
Body: [[I'd be lying if I said your email didn't affect me deeply. And I'd also be lying if I said I haven't thought about you. I've wondered if you've been alright ever since we broke up. You seemed to have the Resurgence and your

University studies. You seemed to have friends, so I wished you the best silently and from a respectful distance.

Your suggestion makes me afraid, Shey. I'm afraid that if I take you there, my feelings for Stok will get mixed up with you somehow. It's a very special place for me. More special than you can imagine.

I have to admit though, and this is what I have meant to tell you for nearly twelve months—I wasn't kind to you, and I'm sorry. I was afraid of hurting you, and in being silent and passive, I hurt you even more. Maybe if I hadn't held back, if I'd opened up more, things could have been different. And I wouldn't be so... scarred.

In other words, I owe you one.

Tonight, after 11, come down Menali Street like you're going to the arboretum. Just as it skirts along Zone H, count seventeen wall panels, then knock. I'll be there.]]

TENTH MONTH, SECOND DAY, 5:55 PM
TO: «Le Namgyal»
FROM: «Shey Choglamsar»
SUBJECT: RE: Your Polemical Diatribe
BODY: [[See you then.]]

"No!" Matho yelled. "Absolutely not."

I looked up.

"I can't ask anyone else to do this," Kish said.

"You don't have to. I'm volunteering!" Matho stomped a small crater into the ground.

I walked up to them. "What's the problem?"

Kish shot me an exasperated look.

"I'm going," Matho said.

Kish cast him a malevolent gaze. "Stand down!"

"Yes ma'am," Matho grumbled.

I cleared my throat.

Kish turned me, her hands on her hips. "It is vitally important to get these computerminds to A2 within the next... seven minutes. Problem is the final stretch into their territory is crawling with deranged. We need a distraction."

I gulped. "A person..."

"Yes, a person." Kish's gaze grew harsher still.

Thoughts stewed in my brain. I pulled at the disparate strands, and they formed an idea.

"Nanites..." I said.

Matho threw up his arms. "Why's he even here, Kish?"

"Shut up, Matho." Kish turned to me. "What are you thinking, Stok?"

"The nanites from Alterra... some of them make lights that float around in the air. Others make this metallic film grow all over everything. Those nanites are clearly not doing that to me, but if the program for those effects is still inside them somewhere, then we can just send them out as our distraction, right?"

I hadn't even finished speaking, and Kish and Matho had both pulled up their computer interfaces and begun sifting through windows.

"Found the one for the lights." Matho smiled. "It's a pretty simple luminescence program."

"A luminescence program they've never seen before." Kish grinned. She turned to her team. "Has anyone ever heard of anyone trying floating lights?"

The team members glanced between themselves, shrugging and shaking their heads.

I looked up desperately at Kish. Let this whole damn trip be worth something to someone. Please.

"Duplicate his nanites and send them out," Kish said.

Matho and couple of others worked furiously at their computer interfaces.

"You better hope this works," Kish muttered just loud enough for me to hear.

I turned my attention to my map overlay, my eyes darting between green dots. The path forward still jumped and stuttered, unable to find a safe route through the deranged.

I closed my eyes.

Please. Please, let it work.

I opened my eyes.

The green dots began to move, slowly at first, then faster and faster.

The line darted, this way and that, and.... It locked.

"Go!" Kish shouted, and we raced down into the next valley and over the next hill. I ranked up alongside Kish and Matho and grinned at them.

"Wipe that smile off your face, kid!" Matho snarled. "Focus on the path."

Indeed. The deranged were already retreating back toward their original positions.

"I told you." Kish turned to me as we plummeted into the valley. "They think thousands of times faster than we do. We survive only by avoiding them."

I turned back to the overlay. The path remained stable. Almost there.

A green dot picked up speed and gained on us.

"Full charge!" Matho roared.

Kish and Matho and the rest of the contingent hurried faster, their top speed. Our small group fanned out, the men carrying computerminds falling to the rear. I dropped back just enough to be in front of them.

"C'mon, c'mon!" I shouted.

A shimmer of demon silver swooped past, a streak of claws and fangs and metallic limbs. The three men carrying computerminds became two.

I turned my attention back to the overlay. Two more green dots came within striking distance.

The red haze of safety appeared before us.

The men behind me surged faster still, a computermind slunk pathetically over each of their necks, sweat and fear splattered over their faces.

Two more flashes of silver behind them, and I feared they'd been lost, but when I turned back, they were still there.

We all hurtled through the red haze and screeched to a halt in front of a giant, metal building.

"Get them downstairs!" Matho shouted.

Kish threw open a door and the two men carried their human cargo into the building's depths.

Matho and the others disappeared. Kish remained, holding the door.

"You going in?" Kish asked.

"Yeah." I started downstairs.

Her hand met my shoulder. "That's the second time you've saved the lot of us. You did good today."

I nodded and walked down the basement steps.

Kish followed, and the doors clanged shut behind us.

I had walked this road before late at night. I'd stayed late at Resurgence meetings, talking until Logic knows when. The only sounds at this time of night were the croaking of gemma toads and the whistling of the wind as it whipped through the still grass.

I understood why they'd come out here. Zone H was by far the easiest to sneak into. Half of me was still convinced that by going in I'd be exposing myself to nanite pathogens, or worse. But Le had seemingly discovered no adverse effects over the course of a year, and I was out of options on all other fronts.

The sleek, rectangular wall slabs plastered with black and yellow tape emerged from the night and formed up along my right.

"One, two, three..."

I must have been completely out my mind. Nostalgic. Still in love. That must have been it. I hadn't gotten over him.

"Fourteen."

I stopped. *I shouldn't be doing this. I should go home and*—

I thought of my father.

"Fifteen, sixteen, seventeen."

I knocked.

At first, nothing.

The slab slid open. Le's face appeared. I inhaled sharply, looked around myself, and hurried inside.

Le slid the slab shut behind me. He wore his novice's robes even here.

We stared at each other momentarily. Tiny green lights danced about. Two of them collided and erupted into a flurry of sparks.

"Hi, Le."

He said nothing, just took off into the forest.

"Not even a greeting?"

He turned back to me, a finger over his lips, his eyes wide.

"Ah," I whispered.

We trekked deeper into the forest, eventually stopping at a downed, moss-covered log. Le sat down and nodded to his side. I joined him.

"I can hear water. Over there." I pointed behind us,

"That'd be the river."

"Maybe we can go see?"

"No," Le said.

I bit my lip.

"I'm sorry." Le sighed. "If you want, you can take a look later. I just... won't go over there."

"Okay..."

"Something wrong with the Resurgence?"

I twisted up my face and stuffed my hands under my thighs. "Yeah. They're... the people rising to the top of the organization... I thought I understood the Resurgence. I thought I knew what they were about. But I don't understand these people. They're deceitful, manipulative, cruel, and so ridiculously stubborn. Nothing you say to them makes any difference. Most of them probably can't even tell you how the scientific method works. They just believe what they've decided they want to believe."

"Like your father," Le said quietly.

My monologue deflated. I should have seen it coming, but I hadn't. All the logic and reason in the world, and I hadn't seen them for what they were until they'd already wrapped their tendrils around me.

"They're like everything we accuse the Monastery of, except they worship the altar of scientific discovery instead of the Divine One."

Le gave me a wan smile.

"I understand now, Le. I'm... sorry for the things I said before."

"I'm sorry, too."

"It was nice. The times we were together, right?"

He smiled more broadly. "Yeah. They were good times."

Another awkward pause.

"The Holy Way is just as insane," Le said. "If not more."

"No kidding. The Resurgence is planning something for the Festival because they've heard the Holy Way's planning a Messenger again. I don't know what though. They've locked me out. I'm not 'trustworthy' anymore. I've talked to 'wrong' people and asked too many 'wrong' questions."

"I heard the Holy Way is planning something bigger than another Messenger this year, too."

"*Bigger*? Seriously?"

"Like I said. Insane."

I kicked at the dirt and tried to catch one of the floating lights, but they scurried away from me. "So, what do we do?"

"The last time I was in this forest, I had plans. I had big, grand, happy plans. I don't want to have plans anymore, Shey. I don't want to think about third ways or new configurations for society—"

I held up my hand. "Wait a sec. Third way? What's that?"

Le swallowed hard. "An idea. The University's idea is that science is right. The Monastery's idea is that the Writ is right. The third way is an idea that neither one is right or wrong. That both are equally valuable, and there are dozens or even hundreds of other 'ways' out there worth exploring."

I leaned back and gripped the log. The dancing lights seemed to leave trailing streaks before my eyes.

So, that was it. Stok had brought Le out here, told him all about this third way, they'd sat by the river and philosophized, dreamed of saving the world's ideological polarization together.

I furrowed my brow. Something didn't add up. I turned to Le, opened my mouth, then stopped. Dark clouds had overwhelmed him. I could feel him sinking into despair.

"Le," I began carefully. "I know this must be a rough subject, but I have to ask. If Stok was so big into this third way, why the hell did he let himself become the Messenger?"

Tears welled up in Le's eyes.

"Oh, I'm sorry— Come here." I scooted closer and wrapped my arm around him. Le's head hit my shoulder and he soaked my wickshirt with tears.

Le sniffed and sat up. "He was convinced that the Asurans kicked our ancestors out for being too ideologically stubborn, and that was the reason we have all these problems today. He wanted to convince them to help us."

I shrugged. "He might still. We don't know what happened to him."

"We know that no Messenger in four hundred years

133

has ever come back. The portal just sits there. It's a religious artifact. Nothing more."

"You don't know that!" I said. "*You* of all people can't
tell me that there isn't even the tiniest part of you that be-
lieves he might come back some day!"

Le looked into my eyes. His frown turned into a grin,
which spread across his face. He laughed, a chuckle at first.
It grew into a full belly roar, and he grabbed at my shoulder to steady himself.

"What?" I asked.

"Shey Choglamsar convincing Le Namgyal to *have
some faith*."

I chuckled, and then I laughed too.

When I settled, I put my hand on his shoulder. "Le,
even if what you think is true, which it might not be, the
best way to respect Stok is to work on building the world
he wanted to live in. Collaboration between the University
and the Monastery can begin with us!"

Le turned to me, and for just a moment, the clouds
around him parted. I saw before me the Le I'd met in the
Bibliotech so many years ago, the Le who I'd done homework with, went on hikes with, before ideology tore us
apart.

"Okay," Le said.

"Awesome!" I squeezed his shoulder. "So... what do we
do first?"

A kick at my side. "Hey Alty, can't you hear the siren?

Divine One, I had gotten so sick of Matho's voice. Not the greatest way to start a day.

I pulled myself up from the pile of cotton on the floor called my mattress. The metallic, bulging biceps before my eyes shocked me for mere milliseconds. And then I remembered. I'd taken the upper body enhancements a month ago. I wondered if I'd ever feel like myself again.

"Alty!"

"I hear you!" My speech was still slurred with grogginess. Orange lights ruptured the space around me. Clanks resounded as metal feet ran up metal stairs.

I jogged to the base of the staircase.

"Rifle, Alty," Matho called down.

"No." I scowled back. I'd made my stance on weaponry abundantly clear.

Matho must have decided he was done harassing me, because he ran down the hall and away.

Tarangar appeared at my side. "You alright?"

I yawned and stretched.

He smiled. "Don't take Matho seriously, Stok."

"I don't."

"You know, if you told Kish about the nickname, she'd probably stop him from saying it."

I shook my head.

We picked up into a run, rushing down the hallways.

"Why do you put up with his shit?" Tarangar shook his head at me. "You've helped us so much! You deserve better."

135

I bit my lip. "I don't, really."

Tarangar frowned. I turned away from his disappointed gaze and rushed away down A5's corridors.

We exited out onto the surface, and I squinted into the sunlight glaring at us from over the horizon. The hazy red wall of warring nanite factions bulged toward us.

I sighed as we ran at it. Matho and a few others had already taken up positions around it. I turned my head and found Tarangar had caught up with me.

"Does this ever end?" I asked.

"No," Tarangar said. "Adding computerminds only decreases the frequency."

I'd been here three months and we'd already done this more times than I could count. We took up positions around the protrusion and used our feeble, un-enhanced brains to assist the computerminds working from below. The wall of red ebbed forward slower and slower. Then it stopped.

The orange lights ceased, and we turned and walked back toward the entrance to the base.

"Hey guys!" A young man by the name of Nohar ran up to us. Not that he looked like a young man with all the enhancements. He just acted young, though I had no idea how he managed to stay that way. "I've decided to start up a Kela tournament."

Tarangar furrowed his brow. "A what?"

Nohar projected a hologram from his synthetic eye. Dice and cards danced before us as we descended into the

136

base. "It's a game. From hundreds of years ago. All the rules are in the computer. Kish gave me permission to replicate the materials."

Tarangar smirked. "Count us in."

Nohar clapped him on the shoulder. "Awesome."

"What do you mean 'us?'" I asked.

Nohar's smile fell.

"You don't want to play?" Tarangar nudged me.

"It's not that, I just never said—"

Tarangar looked at me, not with hostility, but a mix of sadness and fear. He leaned in and whispered into my ear. "The most dangerous thing that can happen to a person on Asura is losing belief in himself. Nohar lives that principle better than any of us. You'll play."

"Stok?" Kish's voice. She stood in the doorway to her office. I hadn't even realized we'd entered this hallway.

"Yeah?"

"A moment."

Fear pierced my heart.

I nodded to Tarangar and Nohar. "See you guys later."

I entered Kish's office, and she closed the door behind me.

"I'd offer you a seat, but—"

I waved away the apology. "It's alright."

Since taking the upper body enhancements, I had grown too heavy for conventional chairs. Especially rusty ones.

"If this is about my refusal to take up weaponry, I'm

afraid—"

"It's not."

"Permission to speak freely."

She raised an eyebrow at me. "Go on."

"After all the help I've given you, I'm more than a bit miffed at the way you and Matho treat me. I mean, look at me, Kish." I held up my engorged, silver hands. "Look at me! Is this human? Seriously? What are we fighting to save?"

"We fight to save humanity," Kish said coldly.

I shot her a scowl. "I don't feel very human anymore."

"You're still human, Stok. We're soldiers. This is war. We've been very lenient with your ideology."

Unbelievable weariness passed over me. I turned toward the door. I wanted to crawl into the pile of cotton that was my bed because a real bed would collapse underneath colossus Stok. "Look, Kish, whatever it is you want, can we just talk about it later—"

"I want you to father my child." She stared at me with cold, hard eyes.

I stood, my mouth agape.

Finally, enough of my neurons began firing again that I regained the capacity for speech. "*What*?"

"It's no secret that Matho is the one I've been preparing. But his arrogance, the way he lets emotion override his judgment..." She shook her head. "You're the only other person on base who wouldn't compromise my leadership."

I put a hand to my forehead. "Divine One, Kish. I'm

gay. You do understand what that means, right?"

Kish rolled her eyes. "Yes, Stok. At least half the people on this base have had experiences with a member of the same sex. Asura soldiers don't let themselves reach our age without producing at least one child. I'm lucky to still have this position. Any man or woman leader of a cell a century ago would have been kicked out by now. I'm still here because– Because no one wants Matho and there's no one else with leadership training. Every human life matters for mere survival now, Stok. I hate to be so blunt about this, but whatever notion of 'human rights' you brought with from Alterra doesn't apply here. A single Asuran life can mean the difference between saving or losing hundreds more. And there are literally only a couple thousand of us left. The stakes are just too high. So yes, gay people reproduce here. We all reproduce here."

I breathed in and out deeply. I closed my eyes.

Le.

I opened my eyes.

"I'm sorry, Kish. I *can't*."

Kish raised an eyebrow. "It's the man you fell in love with, isn't it? The one you told me about from Alterra."

I nodded.

"What was his name again?" For the first time since I'd met her, Kish's expression seemed calm, almost warm.

"Le."

She nodded. "You must miss him."

"You have no idea."

139

The door burst open. I turned and spotted Matho. His eyes spotted me and spewed crimson death. Then they turned to Kish.

"It's C8," Matho said.

Kish slammed a fist on the table and grimaced. "Divine One save us."

"C8?" I asked. "I haven't heard of that one. What kind of base is it?"

"Medical." Matho's face returned to its scowl.

"Maternity." Kish rushed around me to the door.

The next four hours were a blur. Matho screamed at me, and I let him. Kish organized a raiding party. We made contingencies for an extended deployment. A5 would be at risk while we were gone. Voices screamed out commands, and it all washed together, tumbling into a psychotic haze– my life on Asura, my punishment for my arrogance.

We ran across the landscape, over dead hills, along dead rivers. That damned metallic grass grew everywhere. Clusters of evolvers, I'd learned. Not really grass at all.

"First Kela game when we get back," Nohar said.

I must have mumbled a response.

"Tell me about Alterra?" Nohar asked.

I related what I remembered. Nohar listened rapt, chugging along beside me. In the telling, I felt as close to calm as I ever did on Asura. The barren, red-brown hills fell away, and I related yellow sand, and the green-blue river, and Le.

I couldn't help but wonder what Le was up to now. I

often found myself wondering if he'd chosen University or Monastery after I'd left. A part of me hoped, for his sake, that he'd chosen University, maybe found himself falling for a coder, like himself, but one with a more tolerable personality than Shey had possessed. Other times, when I really felt like beating myself up, I imagined Le had chosen Monastery, and had persisted in trying to find that fleeting thing I'd supposedly shown him without really even intending to. It's not that I hadn't known all that stuff I'd told him. I had. It's just that I hadn't put it into words until he'd showed up and needed it explained. I wasn't even really sure why I'd been hanging out in Zone H until then, despite it being relaxing. And it certainly wasn't any fun jumping into that nanite anti-grav field alone.

I found myself tearing up at such thoughts, and then, in a moment, my entire emotional landscape twisted and contorted into fear and the surge of adrenaline. Shouts went up from our group. C8's red barrier wobbled chaotically before me.

We broke into our fastest run. Nohar and I, two of the fastest runners, surged ahead.

"Stay back, Stok!" Kish's voice.

"I'll be fine," I shouted over my shoulder.

"You don't have a rifle, Stok! Fall back!"

I scowled and acquiesced, trailing in her wake.

We burst through the shifting red.

Voices erupted around us. Rifle fire.

"Open fire!" Kish shouted.

Metallic beings clambered about the compound rising meters taller than humans. They tore at buildings, then turned and lunged when they spotted us.

Dozens of scratchy metallic shrills erupted, beating out an off-kilter melody.

"*Inferus*," they chanted.

These deranged came in different sizes than others I'd seen. The ones I'd glimpsed prior had stood four to five meters tall. Many of these stood only two or three meters tall, though they had the same proportions as their larger counterparts.

I spotted a tall one. Its stomach exploded, and shrapnel hurtled toward me. I leapt to the ground and my back blazed with pain. I looked up to the sickening sight of a smaller deranged climbing out of the exploded torso husk of its parent as our soldiers pelted both of them with energy bullets. They shrieked and fell to the ground.

I gazed about the metallic horror.

My mind crashed into a gut-wrenching realization. The deranged had gotten their evolvers into a hospital and maternity ward. I was looking at children and pregnant women whose DNA had been reprogrammed to metamorphose them into creatures who honestly believed that their existence was superior to ours.

A scream went up behind me, one I recognized.

A deranged shrieked with glee, holding Matho in its hand. Silver traced its way over Matho's body.

My heart had never pumped faster. I spotted a rifle on

the ground and grabbed it up. I fired at the thing holding Matho. It shrieked and dropped him to the ground. His body fell like a broken doll.

"Anti-nanogenics!" I shrieked.

All around me were blasts of rifle fire and screaming and shrieks of "*inferus*."

I ran to Matho, but two deranged cut me off, one older and one younger. I could still make out the human forms of their faces. They opened their mouths at me, baring silver razors.

I shot them. My eyes streamed tears.

I trampled their bodies, and searched the ground with my eyes, but Matho was gone. Or was he here, amidst this slick of death at my feet, and he'd already been converted too far to be recognized from any of the other deranged corpses?

I looked about.

He was gone. Or unrecognizable. Lost to the horde of deranged. Lost, like we all were.

Kish's voice pierced my trance. "Fall back!"

I retreated toward her on pure adrenaline instinct. The red wall collapsed inward. The husks of C8's buildings disintegrated and drifted away as though caught up in a breeze.

Kish continued shouting, and we shot deranged as we ran.

"You're holding a rifle," Tarangar said.

I realized now we were running quietly. We were far

from the former site of resistance cell C8. How long had passed since the shrieks of the deranged had faded into the distance? I said nothing.

"Divine One," Nohar said. "That was…"

"That was… beyond horrific," Tarangar said.

"Stok?" Nohar said.

"I'll be fine."

A jerk at my shoulder nearly toppled me mid-stride. Kish pulled me back to the rear of our running contingent.

"Matho," she said. "What happened to Matho?" Cold fire in her eyes.

I shook my head.

Her eyes narrowed. The fire intensified.

She sped forward.

We chased the sunset, running the hundreds of kilometers home to A5.

The day's classes were tedious and dull. Subjects that had seemed beautiful in their endless complexity such as computer programming and genetic recombination theory had dimmed to somber embers.

I kept thinking back to that forest with its floating lights. Such a bizarre experience—my analytical mind knew that the effect was merely clusters of tiny robots generating luminesce and traversing space according to paths determined by random number generators. And yet, the experience had been so much more than that.

Maybe it was my conversation with Lu, the expulsion

of my guilt, jealousy, and self-righteous bitterness. Compassion had washed them away, waves of it crashing over me each time I witnessed Le in Rig, always eating or studying alone.

I tapped at the computer on my desk. The pitter patter of interface sound effects filled the classroom.

What meaning had I found here just days ago? The algorithms and equations had grown tedious and vile. Had my drive to learn, to know, to seek, to strive risen from a yearning so childish and base that it could be shrugged off overnight?

A knock at the door.

The professor continued typing at his interface.

Another knock, harder.

The professor stood, still typing. He initiated a compilation sequence, then finally turned his attention away from his computer and walked to the door.

Three men in police uniforms stepped inside our classroom. Two stood at the door. One of them drew the professor toward his desk. The two of them mumbled for some time, then turned around.

"We're here for Candidate Shey," the policeman said.

The whole class stopped their typing and looked at me. I stood. "What's the matter?"

The man's face was cold. "We need you to come with us."

My peers' eyes followed me out of the room. I followed the police. I knew better than to open my mouth. There's one thing that my dad was good for—taught me when it was in my best interest to restrain words that would be more trouble than they were worth to utter.

Thoughts churned through my head. What did they think they knew? I wished I had my computer. I wasn't strong or agile like Le and Stok. I'd decided not to elect a tournament at the Festival. It had seemed like the right decision at the time, but I'd been growing to regret it, especially after hearing about the morning exercises at Monastery. I had to admit, those sounded kind of fun.

Damn. I *needed* my computer, my connection to the web of stored human thought, the world where *I* could make a difference.

The police led me out of the University and down the main road. I received more gawking stares and did my best to ignore them. The police headquarters rose up in the distance, but to my surprise, we passed it.

I almost spoke up, but I decided keeping my mouth shut was still best.

We approached the hospital, a big white building of interlocking rectangles, and we entered.

Fear struck me. Were my new enemies among the Resurgence really so powerful?

We walked right past reception. They took me down a long hallway, and we passed through two large, metallic doors, a biohazard emblem emblazoned upon them. We turned. Halfway down this new hall, we stopped at a door to a room.

Two of the policemen took up posts, and one of them entered.

He turned and beckoned me inside. I took a moment, breathing in and out as carefully as I could, and then entered. My heart pounded out of my chest. I felt the beginnings of tremblings in my hands and shoved them behind me back.

"On the bed," the policeman said.

The room was white. No window. It looked like an ordinary doctor's office—cabinets, a counter with swabs and gauze, a bed with a layer of paper over it. Nothing unusual.

I sat on the edge of the bed and looked at him. "And now?"

"We wait for the doctor."

I found some meager bit of courage within me. "You know my dad's a member of the House of Analytics, right?"

Second thing Dad's been useful for today. He's on a roll.

The policeman plucked a small computer off his hip, tapped at its interface a few times, and handed it to me.

I nearly dropped it—a general order to detain me and Le, and then to run deep nanogenic scans on the both of us. The order had been passed down from the chief of police, who had created it at the request of one Surat Choglamsar. My father.

Rage erupted, exploding from chest into all my extremities. My lips and eyes quirked. I carefully handed the policeman his computer back. He eyed me carefully, as though perhaps I were a time bomb or an animal about to go rabid. He seemed almost sad when we returned to muted non-interaction.

I decided to let anger seethe within me for whatever time I was stuck here with them.

The door opened, and the doctor entered. He was short, had curly grey hair and glasses. He wore the white robes of a doctor and held a computer tablet, a rather large one, the size of a cafeteria tray.

"You must be Shey," the doctor said. "I'm Doctor Akot."

"I'll wait outside," the policeman said.

"Wait!" I shouted. I turned to the doctor. "Show me your credentials."

The doctor activated his enormous computer, and a doctor's license appeared a few button taps later. I scanned it for many moments, looking for errors or omissions. The policeman crossed his arms and sighed. I ignored him and continued my visual scan. I reached the end, and, having found nothing, and conceded that, at least on paper, this doctor appeared legitimate.

The policeman left, leaving me alone with Akot.

"Do you know what a nanogenic scan is?" The doctor asked.

I rolled my eyes. "Yes, just please get this over with."

They would find the nanites and I would be sent to quarantine. Couldn't even guess what would happen after that. Quarantine protocol hadn't been invoked in centuries.

"Take off your clothes."

I stripped down to my underwear and socks and sat on the bed once more.

The doctor pursed his lips. "I'm afraid the order says that it must be a deep scan at one hundred percent strength." He paused. "You must wear nothing."

You just had to humiliate me too, Dad, didn't you?

I threw my underwear and socks in the pile on the floor.

"Lie down," the doctor said.

I did.

He held the enormous computer between us. Lights passed over me, greens and blues mostly. I closed my eyes and tried to imagine I was somewhere else. Even there, the faint glow of the scan penetrated my eyelids, seeping into my fantasy. My skin tingled and itched.

The light ceased.

"You can get dressed now," the doctor said.

I grabbed up my clothes and pulled them back on.

"Well?"

"No nanites. You're clean."

Huh. So much for that. My brief victory elation was quashed by another thought—I'd have to deal with Dad.

The doctor exited the room. I heard him tell the policeman the results of the scan. After I finished dressing, I exited too. The doctor had disappeared, but the three police remained.

Muted screaming erupted from a room down the hall. Two police stationed outside another door opened it and ran inside.

"—they're fucking harmless, just *listen* to—"

Le.

Two of the policeman guarding my door ran to the other. The third, the one who'd been in the room with me, escorted me down the hall, and out through the metallic double doors with the biohazard sign. We stopped.

"You are free to go," the policeman said. "Thank you for your cooperation."

He disappeared behind the double doors.

I marched out of the hospital.

My feet took over for me. My rational mind faded into the background, and I was feeling, gloriously feeling, but the emotions jostled me, turbulent and chaotic. Rage and betrayal took primacy. They propelled me forward.

From the top of the hill bordering Zone B, I spotted the University in the distance. I used to think it was beautiful. I saw it now as a giant, festering cyst upon the land.

My legs propelled me further, down the hill and toward an opulent, ornate building of sandstone fronted by a tower of stairs. The biggest, grossest, most malignant cyst of them all.

Parliament.

My muscles rippled and tensed. I stood up and huffed. I grabbed the I-beam and tugged at it again, gritting my teeth. It gave a bit, and I strained harder.

The beam lurched free, and I took a few steps back to catch myself. The thing was huge, maybe four or five meters long. Rust had taken its edges. I hauled it up onto my shoulder and heard the familiar clang of metal against metal behind me.

"You good?" I called back to Nohar, who crouched over his own stuck I-beam on the other side of the room.

"I'm good."

I took off down the stairs, and Tarangar stepped aside to let me through.

"Three more," I told him.

"Gotcha." He waited for me to pass then rushed by.

I hurried down two more flights, ran across the compound, and tossed the beam into the heap we'd made.

Kish stood beside it tapping at her computer.

"How much longer?" I asked.

She shook her head. "At least another five minutes."

"Time enough for one more run then." I took off.

"Hey!" she shouted.

I turned.

"Make sure the others get out of the building instead. We don't want to become another C8."

The sounds of children's screams distorting into a hollow metal roar filled my mind. Just momentarily. "That won't happen here."

"Then get them out of the building," Kish said. "We can scrap the rest."

I nodded and ran off. I opened the door to the warehouse and ran inside.

"Hey guys," I yelled up the mesh metal stairwell, "you coming?"

An enormous clanging crash was my only response.

"Nohar?" I called out. I ran up the stairs. "Kish wants us out of here, guys."

Fear rushed my veins. Did I still have veins? I still asked those kinds of questions too much, despite long talks with Tarangar on the subject. It turned out, unsurprisingly, that doubting one's humanity was a common psychological condition on Asura.

Six months of hearing Kish tell me that the enhancements were temporary had grown hollow. Something always needed to be done—something that required more speed, more strength. It never ended.

Another crash sounded.

"Stok!" Nohar's voice.

Tarangar yelled in pain.

I hurried up the stairs faster, and alighted in the attic, where we'd been harvesting I-beams. A mesh of metal and wire lay in a wreck atop Tarangar. Wind blew in from a hole in the roof.

"Divine One, Tarangar." I ran for the pile, where Nohar stood, chucking aside enormous hunks of debris.

"Tarangar took the wrong beam," Nohar said. "Brought the whole ceiling infrastructure down."

He lay on his back, his lower half pinned beneath tons

of rubble. The floor creaked ominously.

I took a spot alongside Nohar and joined him in throwing away ceiling detritus.

"You guys get out of here," Tarangar said.

I laughed. "You kidding? And let you beat me by three games of Kela?"

"Is Kish going to start without us?" Nohar grunted as he threw an I-beam into the wall.

"No," I said. "But I'd bet the computerminds will."

"All the more reason for you guys to get out of here!" Tarangar dug his claws into the floor, pulled on himself and screamed.

"Quit it!" Nohar said. "Just wait a damn minute."

Unnatural groaning noises emanated from the floor.

"Guys—" Tarangar said.

"Shut up!" Nohar and I shouted in unison. We tag-teamed a particularly large beam and heaved it into the corner. We moved on to the metal mesh holding Tarangar down. We each took one side of an I-beam and levered the mesh off the floor.

Tarangar grunted and clawed himself free.

Nohar and I ran to him, each of us grabbing a shoulder, and hauled him down the stairs.

A deafening metal crash resounded, the sound of the upper floor giving way.

Nohar and I dragged Tarangar away from the warehouse and back toward our pile. I waved to Kish, and she signaled back. The familiar hiss of nanites erupted from behind us. The warehouse wrenched, twisted and granulated, its component molecules ground apart. The red wall of computermind nanites retracted over the space where the warehouse had stood.

We'd lost storage space, but also reduced the surface area needed to protect us from the evolvers–and that meant we wouldn't need as many computerminds to keep us safe. Kish had told me privately that this retraction of land had been going on for two hundred years. A5 started out about five times bigger than it was now. The records said it had grown a bit in its first few decades. But for the last two hundred, the deranged had made incremental gains month over month, year over year.

Kish eyed the three of us. "Get him to the infirmary."

"Yes ma'am."

"And Stok?" Kish eyed me. "Can you come to my office when you're done?"

Awkward hesitation sent electric ripples through my musculature. "Yeah... sure."

"See you soon."

I carried Tarangar off, alongside Nohar. We descended into the A5's subterranean halls.

"Why you so anxious around the chief?" Nohar turned to me. "You are the father, right?"

My face flushed. All this metal and muscle, yet embarrassment could still overtake me.

"Dude!" Tarangar slapped Nohar in the back of the head. "Stok's gay. Show some respect."

"Sorry, Stok." Nohar frowned and looked away.

That made me feel good and guilty. It wasn't Nohar's fault I hadn't been talking about my imminent parenthood.

"Hey," I said, drawing his attention. I managed a weak smile. "Don't worry about it. There's nothing wrong with asking."

It was hard to tell from looking at him, but Nohar was nineteen, just like me. He maintained a kind of childishness unique amongst the soldiers of A5. He seemed more interested in games than romantic coupling, whereas most of the guys and girls our age still had fully human bodies and were busy 'doing their duty for the species' in their free time. I doubted any of them found it a chore.

We dropped Tarangar off in the infirmary, and I walked the crimson hallways to Kish's office.

It had only been six months, but already my life on Alterra felt like a dream or distant memory, a lost time when adventure had been an intriguing option and the ability to choose love was a birthright rather than an unattainable luxury.

I still thought about Le, about what his life might be like now, and especially about whether or not he'd moved on. Especially now, when I was alone, my thoughts tended to coalesce around what I had given up in order to come here. The people I'd wanted to help likely thought me dead, and now I had a whole new family, of sorts, to help out of a much more precarious situation. If only my fellow Alterrans knew...

155

I knocked on Kish's office door.

"Come in."

I entered and propped myself up before her desk.

"You don't have to be so formal, you know."

I nodded, trying to relax, but my muscles wouldn't cooperate.

She shook her head. "I keep forgetting to requisition that chair..."

"Not a problem," I replied, choking on the words.

"I'm sorry I mentioned C8 earlier. It was careless of me." Her expression fell to dismay and regret. "I-I need to be more conscientious and less... harsh... for him." She righted her posture and looked me in the eyes. "It won't happen again."

"Not a problem." I grabbed the door handle.

"Stok, wait."

"Yes?"

"I didn't realize that... our having been together would make you so uncomfortable around me."

I paused.

"I mean, it makes sense, now that I think about it. I just—" She sighed, not seeming to know what to say next.

Exasperated, I closed my eyes. I steadied my breathing. It took all my willpower to look at her and speak. "I respect you and I trust you with my life, Kish. I did what I had to do to help you, because you're my friend and I care about you and everyone else in A5." I paused and took another deep breath. "I keep telling myself that, but I still feel horrible. I just can't—"

"You worry about how Le will react, don't you?"

"Yeah."

"And the fact that this is how we have to do things on Asura is probably never going to help, is it?"

"Probably not."

"Well, tell you what, Stok. Our son is going to need parents who love him, no matter how much of a wreck his world is. So, if you can find a way to be in the same room with me, for him, then I'll get us all to Alterra so that you, me, *and* Le can be a part of his life. Sound like a deal?"

"Deal." I chuckled. "I'll bet you don't even remember where you picked me up."

Kish mimicked my words with mocking babble, and we both laughed.

"Is nineteen young to have a child on Alterra?" she asked.

"Yeah."

"Did you ever imagine being a parent... before?"

I shook my head and rubbed at my temples. "No. I never really thought about it."

"Especially with C8 gone, our kids need all the help they can get."

I raised my hands. "I've handled every other task you've thrown at me. Parenthood? What the hell. Hey, I got one. Next you can have me build nanite shield walls, except they'll be as good as computerminds. How about that?"

Kish furrowed her brow. "Nanite shield walls?"

I lowered my gaze. My eyes drifted to Kish's desk, rounded the room and made their way back to her. "Yeah. We had them on Alterra. I could have sworn I'd told you about them."

"No... I'm pretty sure you didn't."

I crossed my arms. "Well, yeah. I mean, they were invented three hundred and fifty years ago. I figured that a computermind was way more advanced."

Kish picked up her pad and opened programs frantically. "Why did you even invent such a thing?"

I rubbed my hands through my hair, wracking my brain for the relevant history lesson. "When the avatars arrived four hundred years ago, they brought a bunch of nanites with them they didn't understand, and they were afraid of them, so they had their few programmers code them to stay within certain areas.

"At first, people would just sit around in shifts making sure that the nanites stayed put, but after a few generations, we somehow built a bunch of walls so people wouldn't have to constantly monitor them."

"Divine One save us," Kish threw her computer onto her desk. "You had walls that could hold back nanites, *and you're just telling me now?!*"

I threw up my hands. "I swear, I thought they were inferior tech! I mean, I'm not even really used to thinking of them as technology at all. They're just big hunks of metal."

She marched up to me, her eyes ablaze. "Nanites can

go over and under walls. There's got to be more to it. How do they work?"

I squinted and bunched up my lips. "I don't know."

"*What?!*"

"I studied for Monastery! Programming and computers were never my forté. You want Le for that. I'm sure he'd be able to tell you all about them. I do remember..."

Her eyes flooded with hope. "Yes?"

"Le did talk about them once. Something about a metal on Alterra being important. Something about, um, generating a special kind of EM field. When you line the wall slabs up, make a circle, it makes the field as big as the whole perimeter. Really small things, like nanites, can't get through the field, but large things pass through easily. Something about quantum... um, gravity? Maybe?"

"And?"

"That's it."

"That's it?" Kish leveled a malevolent gaze at me. "So, Le said, 'the walls create a kind of EM field that changes quantum gravity using a metal we mine here on Alterra.'"

"Right."

"And then you said..." She rolled her hand.

I bit my lip and squinted. "I think I said, 'let's make out.'"

"Ugh! You men are *pigs!*" She shoved me out of her office and slammed the door in my face.

"Hope you don't tell our son that!" I yelled.

I started to walk away. I sighed and knocked on her

door instead.

She opened it a crack.

"Who do I talk to about quantum grav—?"

"Agra. Lab Two."

"Thanks."

"No problem."

There was a rhythm in my step as I strode down the hallways toward A5's laboratories. For the first time in six months, Alterra didn't seem quite so far away.

The door buzzed and the Legislative Security Officer beside me pulled it open. I stormed into dad's office. He sat at his desk reading a computer display. He stared at it and tapped at a few buttons, then swiped a window into oblivion.

He wore that black suit he was so fond of, and the orange tie that he was constantly mentioning was his favorite.

The door buzzed behind me, announcing itself sealed.

"What the *fuck*, dad?"

Dad shot out of his chair. "Watch your tongue, young man! Show some respect for this office!"

"Respect..." I let out a laugh. "You talk about respect. Do you have any idea what you've just done?"

His eyes narrowed and he scowled. "I've just made you and this city much safer, you ungrateful little shit. Do *you* have any idea how lucky you are not to be infected?"

"The ones in Zone H don't infect people! Conduct

some fucking experiments like a *real* scientist and find out the truth. The evidence is just sitting there, waiting to be discovered."

"And how do you explain your ex-boyfriend then?" Dad crossed his arms and scowled. "Le's always been a bad influence on you. The day he broke up with you was the best day of your life, and you've been whining about it like a spoiled little brat ever since. When are you going to grow up, Shey?"

Fury erupted, spewing out of me. "I've wanted to say this for so long. Fuck you, dad. Fuck your enormous house, your stupid rules, and your narrow-minded, selfish 'concern,' too."

He strode across the room, fists clenched. A sharp jerk of motion from his side, and pain blossomed across my face. Force toppled me. I stumbled, fell on my hands and knees, and tasted bitter iron in my mouth.

Dad had punched me. He'd punched his own son in the face.

I picked myself up slowly, carefully. Dad stood at the window now, facing outside.

"Get your shit out of my house," he said.

"Gladly." I spat blood on his carpet.

He strode to his desk and tapped a button. The door buzzed and swung open.

Legislative Security pulled me out of his office by the arm. They held their grip all the way to the entrance. For the duration of the trip, I screamed at the top of my lungs, for every member of the House of Analytics to hear, that Representative Choglamsar had failed me as a father and as a decent human being.

Kish descended the staircase into Lab Two. Her facial features sloshed momentarily as the heat hit her. "Whoa! Must be at least thirty degrees in here!"

"Thirty-three," I said.

"They're working on thermal reactivity in the next chamber." Agra stood beside me, a short woman with a slim physique.

Kish joined the two of us at our table full of holographic projections and mathematical gibberish. Well, gibberish to me anyway. She nodded to my sweat-drenched shirt. "You could take that off, you know."

"I'm fine." I was the only guy on base with the upper body enhancements who wore a shirt. I'd made it myself from scraps, not wanting to bother anyone else with the task.

Kish crossed her arms and stared into the sea of incomprehensible gibberish in front of us. "How long have we been at this?"

"Two months," Agra said flatly.

Her lips traced the words, and she shook her head.

Agra looked up from her computer. Her ocular implants met our eyes. "We have good news, today. The best news. We've got all the basic physics of the walls worked out. An EM field tuned exactly to the right frequency interacting with iron ore that has been exposed to a sustained metaxic field—"

I snapped my fingers. "Right! They dug it up from under the Monastery. I remember that now."

Agra stared at me. I found it hard to read her ocular implants. Her rotating holographic pupils didn't squint or narrow.

"Sorry," I said.

She continued. "The good news is that we have plenty of iron. And even if we didn't, we could generate it with nanites. The bad news is that it will take sixteen years of exposure to a sustained metaxic field in order for the iron to gain the desired properties."

Kish frowned. "Sixteen years? Is there any way to speed that up?"

Agra shook her head. "No. It's a quantum property, not a physical one. The iron needs sustained metaxic exposure for sixteen years at least. Eighteen, optimally."

Kish nodded to Agra. "Get started right away." She turned to me. "Stok?"

"Yeah?"

"My office."

I followed her up the stairs. I'd learned her gait and could tell she was anxious. It was so funny. I'd never noticed the physical details of women's bodies before. And yet, with this woman carrying my child, I had become compelled to notice every little detail, not in a lustful way, but protectively. My physical care sensitivity had been tuned to overdrive. How was she feeling? Was she eating enough? Was she overexerting herself?

And now at five months in, she was starting to show.

Her reaction to Agra surprised me. I thought she'd be much happier than this.

She led me into her office, sat down at her chair, and exhaled heavily.

"How you feeling?" I asked.

"I'm fine."

She grinned up at me. "You remember when we first met? Our first conversation in this room?"

"Divine One, it feels like forever ago." I shook my head. "I was so confused. So naive."

"You weren't that bad. A story for a story, remember? Tarangar and now countless others are alive today because of your prototype nanites."

I nodded, then watched as her demeanor dropped and she stared over my shoulder into the wall behind me. Fine, I'd bite.

"So..." I looked directly at her. "Why aren't you more excited about the walls?"

Kish frowned, and sighed, then nodded to the door.

I opened it a bit, checked around, then shut it.

"We're good," I said.

She kept her voice low. "Best projections have us abandoning A5 in about six years, maybe seven or eight if we're really lucky."

I crossed my arms. "Then let's pull in all our resources.

Merge A2, A6 and A8 into A5."

She pursed her lips. "I thought of that. I ran the projections for making any one of those into our greatest fortification yet. Those only get up to about a decade in the best of circumstances. The energy expenditure would be outrageous, and any number of things could go wrong with transporting all those people and their equipment. The projection always comes out the same—a last stand, eventual ruin. Our being spread out forces the evolvers to spread themselves thinner, too. But we're on the losing side of this war, and every leader of every cell knows it. We need those walls now, Stok. Not in sixteen years."

I nodded, my mind reaching the obvious conclusion. "Alterra."

"Yeah."

"What about the quantum distortion around the portal you told me about?"

"I've started the computerminds on cracking the computers in the ruins of the facility that sealed the portal, but it will take time. We may even need to send a team in."

"I want to lead the team."

Fear traced its way across Kish's face.

I decided to answer the question neither of us wanted to voice. "Father or not, it sounds like he won't have much of a future unless I do this."

Kish nodded. "I'll let you know if they decide they need human hands for the job."

I held up my own before me, long, gnarled things glistening with silver, my muscles all engorged and bubbly and hard as metal. I remembered when this had seemed fun, when my strength and speed had seemed cool. Then I'd been to C8.

I looked at my hands and wondered if my son would recognize me as belonging to the same species as him. Would Le recognize me, or turn away repulsed?

I turned my hands to Kish. "Are these really still human?"

She gulped and nodded. "Yes, Stok. You're very, very human."

"I'll wait in operations until they make the call."

Kish nodded, and I left her office, shutting the door carefully behind me.

It's funny how many of my possessions I'd taken for granted. How I'd taken space itself for granted.

I entered my bedroom and saw it with new eyes. Before it had been computers, a desk, a bed, a closet, and a variety of emotional attachments. What lay spread out before me now was a complex math problem involving numerous objects, each with a 'value' (how useful the thing would be to me outside this structure) and a 'cost' (how much of a liability the thing presented in terms of its weight and bulkiness for a life on the run).

I found that the vast majority of my possessions fell into the 'low value, high cost' category. An important revelation for me indeed.

I grabbed my old backpack out of the closet, the one I had used in secondary school. I tossed my handheld computer into it, three pairs of underwear, three wickshirts and an extra pair of sandals.

"Honey?" Mom appeared at the door. "Is everything alright?"

"I'm sure dad will tell you all about it when he gets home."

"Oh dear. Well, you know how your father can be—"

"For fuck's sake mom, he's an asshole. He's an asshole to you. He's an asshole to me. He's an asshole to all of River Province when they're not watching what he's doing."

"Shey, this is hardly a productive attitude. I'm sure he was just upset."

"He punched me in the face, mom! Stop making excuses for him!" I grabbed up my backpack and pushed past her through the door.

She said nothing. I turned back. She stood at the top of the stairs wearing a pouty expression.

"So... you're leaving me too?"

I sighed. "I can only stand up for myself, mom. I can't stand up for both of us. Not anymore. Goodbye."

I marched out the door.

I found a cafe with long hours. It was still only three, but I wanted somewhere I could stay until late.

I ordered the cheapest drink on the menu and took a seat, happily leeching their network connection. I hacked into the University private network and after four frustrating hours, successfully unlocked the protected archives that contained the documentation for nanite code, untouched for centuries.

It amazed me how, after four hundred years, the fundamental principles of programming and good code design really hadn't changed at all. The more I read about nanite code, the more intrigued I became. They had all the same logical control structures, the same potentials as any other computer. They were just smaller, and their programming interface operated on the structure of matter itself.

Dinner time drew closer and my stomach growled, but I ignored it, lost in my computational reverie.

At ten, the cafe closed and I left. I walked to the University, then around it, past the Monastery hill—the Festival grounds were almost complete—and back to the main road. I veered left at the river, following Menali Street.

I glanced at my computer. Ten thirty.

Close enough.

I snuck into Zone H.

What did Stok show you, Le?

I made my way toward the river. Surprisingly, the ground rose. That was interesting. I'd thought the entire riverbank to be flat.

I crested the top of the hill and looked out. It was a spectacular view. The river lapped at the shore below and stretched out, perhaps a mile across. On the opposite bank were still grass patches and wanwan trees. The sand rose up into enormous dunes, the desert stretching on and away who knew how far.

One day we'd collect enough resources to fuel rockets and satellites, then we'd know what Alterran topography really looked like.

I guess it had been silly to think that the people of the Monastery didn't want us to accomplish that. I bet they did, they just had different priorities, priorities that to them, were just as important as rockets and satellites were to me.

I pulled out my computer.

"Please let them be quantum entangled..." I muttered. I smiled, and snatched up a glowing light as it passed through my field of vision. "You guys are awesome!" I said to it, feeling more than bit silly, but happy nonetheless.

"Can I transmit code via quantum entanglement?" I asked aloud. I turned to my computer and rephrased my question in the form of code. One of the lights before me turned from green to red. I hit another button, and all the lights of the forest updated to match their friend.

Fist pump. "That would be a 'yes.'"

"So, I just need to find the IDs of the ones inside Le's body... Jackpot!" I smiled and continued typing.

I unpacked a data bundle inside one of the nanites and—jackpot! About fifty nanite programs along with documentation. Now I just needed to find something communication related. Perhaps they could write messages on the walls of Le's cell or something.

Just six programs in, though, I found a program I couldn't believe. It sounded dangerous—insane, even. But I had to try. I programmed the nanites to target me, and then Le. I took a few deep breaths, and punched the button to execute the program. I gulped and clenched my eyes shut. I didn't hear anything. Was the program working?

Hey Le?

A response rang out in my ear. *Wow, nice. Now I'm hearing voices in my head. They'll really believe I'm not a fanatic now.*

Le, it's me. Shey.

Silence.

Shey?

Yeah, it's me. I linked our thoughts.

You... what?

The nanites are quantum entangled. It's how they network. Anyway, I'm sorry about what happened to you. It's my father's fault. He must have decoded our emails.

The nanites are in my brain?!

And your ear.

Shey.

Yeah?

I forgive you for the quarantine thing. That's not really your fault. But you put nanites in my brain?

I think they were already there. I put them in my brain, too.

There's no way this is safe.

I don't have a choice. Dad kicked me out of the house.

I'm homeless. And I'm pretty sure the Resurgence is done with me too.

Oh, Shey. I'm really sorry—

Right now I'm more worried about you.

I'm fine. They've got me alone in a cell. They slide food and water in. So much for us bringing the two sides together, right?

I let out a small laugh.

I wish I could do something.

The first step is to get you out of quarantine. I'll work on a way to break you out. During the Festival is our best bet.

They're going to keep guards on me during the Festival, Shey.

Of course, but after what happened last year, most of them will probably be on the other side of the city. They might even have another disaster to deal with. I think the Resurgence is planning something big. I never found out what it was. Ooh...

Oh no. I recognize that tone.

If the University's been taken over by the Resurgence, then there should be something about their plans in the computer system. I'll just hack in and find out what they're up to! I mean, my University career is over. What have I got to lose?

And then what?

... I don't know.

Great.

I'll work on it! I've got all the time in the world now.

Sure. Let me know when you've got something more concrete. Hey, you can turn these things off, right?

Yeah.

Okay. Well, 'bye.'

I laughed. *Bye, Le.*

A pathetic plan indeed. Two ex-boyfriends against the ideological opposition of their entire society, one of them homeless and the other in quarantine.

Somehow though, it didn't seem so bad. I leaned back on my elbows, looked up at the stars, and smiled.

I wish I were home with Le.

I typed out the next access code and the panel buzzed again. Tarangar to my left, Nohar to my right. Shots of nanogenic pathogen rounds pierced the air, sizzling into the metallic screams of their targets.

I typed out another code. Failure.

The room was familiar crimson metal, but the walls, ceiling, and floor were streaked with rust and decay. The building groaned decrepitly.

Another code. Failure.

"Deranged are getting awfully dense," Nohar called out. More pulses and sizzling screams.

Another code.

I said a silent prayer.

Success appeared on my overlay.

"Thanks be the Divine One!" I roared.

"So we can get out of here?" Tarangar turned to me

only momentarily between the expulsion of rounds.

I picked up my rifle and took the window on the opposite side of the room. "No. It means we have to wait for the download to finish. It's at fourteen percent."

"We can't wait for it," Tarangar shouted.

"We can't wait another twenty seconds?"

"No. We need to go now."

I picked off seven deranged. I lowered my rifle and watched them shudder and writhe on the ground. These creatures could still feel pain, and that filled me with such a tumult of emotions. Alas, to them I was merely *homo sapiens inferus*, an infection that needed to be eradicated.

I'd watched them convert a building full of pregnant women and children into screeching metallic horrors. I'd seen the look in an infected Matho's eyes as he'd fallen to the ground, a terror purer than any I'd witnessed.

I raised my rifle and picked off twelve more from my perch.

The enhancements had increased my speed, my agility, my visual acuity, my ability to target and snipe. I had to wonder, had they taken empathy from me as well? Was I now a metallic killing machine in the vague guise of a human, no better than *homo sapiens superus* after all?

Did I deserve to take this data home to A5? Did I deserve to go home to Alterra at all?

One hundred percent.

I ran back to the computer podium between Tarangar and Nohar, ripped the destructor patch from my pocket, and slammed it onto the pillar.

"Out!" I shouted. "Go!"

The three of us took the five flights of stairs in seconds. "We've got deranged in the building!" Nohar announced. Indeed, the green dots on my overlay were splotched overtop my position.

We came halfway down the first floor staircase and opened fire on the shrieking waves of deranged. Tarangar lobbed a nanogenic grenade into the center of the room and we backed up the stairs.

The grenade erupted and the building shook. Sizzling and crackling filled the air, and hundreds of deranged shrieked. I winced at the sound.

The path on my overlay stabilized. We had a way out.

"Wait for it," Nohar said, referring to the malevolent nanite haze the grenades had left. A risky move. Would the path to safety still be there when the haze dissipated?

"C'mon." Tarangar shifted his weight. "C'mon!"

"Now!" Nohar shouted. We rushed down the stairs and out of the building, the shrieks of the deranged growing ever closer.

"Stay close!" I surged forward. I barely broke a sweat, but Nohar and Tarangar strained to keep up with me.

"Whoa, whoa!" I had just stepped onto a hill, when I looked up to discover its grass evaporating. The hill itself wobbled. Its top flattened out and it continued flattening. I veered left around its periphery.

"Reroute!" I shouted to Nohar and Tarangar.

Nohar joined me on my right, but Tarangar had rushed up the hill anyway, and stumbled confusedly as an enormous wave of terraforming evolvers hurtled toward him.

"Tarangar!" I shouted. "Nohar, go!" I pushed him. I broke the path and ran back for Tarangar.

Tarangar careened down the hillside, the terraforming evolver haze at his heels.

He shouted out for me, and I pulled him to safety.

The terraformers dissipated. The hill was now a plain. Deranged shrieks grew imminently closer.

"You alright?" I asked.

Tarangar's eyes lilted back and he collapsed.

"Divine One damn it, Tarangar!"

I hauled him up onto my shoulders and ran.

"What's going on back there?" Nohar's voice in my ear.

"I think Tarangar's been hit with terraformers."

"Shit."

"And I'm out of anti-nanogenics."

"Falling back to your position."

Nohar appeared in the distance, and I slowed to meet him. Nohar pulled off his pack and took out his medical kit. I watched green dots gain on our position from behind us.

"Done," Nohar said.

We took off running, myself significantly slowed.

"What the—?" Nohar said.

I saw it too. The deranged were... retreating.

"Have they ever done that before?" I asked.

Nohar shook his head, eyes wide. "No. Never."

We ran the rest of the way back to A5 and dropped Tarangar off in the infirmary.

Kish lay in a bed on the far side of the room. She'd been spending more and more time here. Her belly had grown significantly. The reality that I would be a father sank in more and more with every day. Joy at the prospect surged within my heart alongside sadness at the horrible world he would be born into. Though I had found no love in helping Kish with her community responsibilities, I'd found love in the care and protection of my mate and off-spring. Somehow, that prospect also eased the quandary of my humanity.

I walked to her bedside and grabbed her hand.

"Did you get it?" she asked.

I nodded.

"You guys did great, Stok."

"Now comes the hardest part. Once the portal's open, the deranged will try to get to Alterra."

"We'll make a plan later." Her eyes grew intense. She clasped my hand harder. "Stok..."

"Yeah?"

"Even if the computerminds get the specs together sooner, wait for Mox. Please."

I nodded.

A howling scream pierced the infirmary.

Kish tried to pull herself up on her elbows, but a nurse

asked her calmly to lie back down.

I dropped Kish's hand and ran across the room.

"Get him sedated!" A doctor shouted.

"I've got one arm," an orderly said. "Get someone else with upper enhancements in here!"

A grabbed Tarangar's other arm. A pile of brownish dirt lay on the ground at the foot of the bed. Tarangar's light skin had taken on brownish pigment, not the brown of my skin, but a deeper brown with the reddish tint of soil.

"Thanks," the orderly said.

Tarangar squirmed and surged. His feet flew about and he howled again.

"Can we get some help here?!" a doctor shouted. Staff flew about the infirmary.

Tarangar's eyes grew lucid, just as his skin rippled and began peeling, turning browner. His muscles withered and the silver flaked off along with hunks of his skin.

"Stok?" Tarangar looked up at me.

"Yeah, buddy. I'm here."

He hurtled up and puked mud onto himself.

"Nanogenic pathogen containment team!" the doctor shouted.

"Stok..."

"I'm right here."

"I got eight months more than I deserved because of you. I made too many sloppy mistakes to survive this long."

"You're gonna get more than eight months."

"You're such a good friend." Tarangar wheezed. "You

said you don't deserve to get Le back, to go home, but you do. I say so, okay buddy?"

He writhed against my hold, yelled and panted. His legs fell away to dirt, and the line of rot spread up his torso.

"Go home, Stok. You put that Monastery and University *and us* together because I say you're the right person to do it, all right?"

A doctor pulled at my hands. "Let him go!"

I did.

Tarangar stared at me as the rest of him collapsed into flecks of gray-brown dirt, a heap on the table.

A hazmat team rushed into the room and locked down Tarangar's deathbed.

I meandered back to Kish, where she pulled herself up of the table. We hugged.

"I'm sorry," Kish said. "He and I were the first two people you met here, huh?"

"Yeah." Tears slipped down my face.

I pulled back.

"I'll wait for Mox," I said. "I promise."

I thought that sitting on sand would have been a lot more comfortable than this. My lower back felt sticky and I was sure I'd gotten sand down my underwear. The University wall I was leaning against had decidedly not been designed for comfort.

The sun roasted me, gazing down from the center of the sky. Waves of heat rippled off the desert. And I sat, my computer interface before me.

Stories and vids had always made out hacking to be an exciting endeavor. Breaking through firewalls, rerouting traffic around monitoring hotspots amidst furious typing and encroaching authorities.

The reality was far less grand.

I sat against the far outside wall of the University triangle. As far as I knew, there were no imminently encroaching authorities to run from. Even if the a University official was paying attention, they probably wouldn't give my activity a second thought. As far as they could tell, I was—I checked my proxy profile again—Fera Raighar, an initiate logging in remotely from wherever the Atharva Expedition had camped out. I'd heard stories of a technology called geolocation, but we possessed no satellites. No one could discover that I was just outside the University instead of a couple hundred kilometers north of the city.

I pulled down huge swaths of encrypted data effortlessly. And decoding encryptions? Been there, done that.

I yawned. Not much to do but sit here and bask in being sweaty and itchy.

I twitched my head. Was I hearing voices? Must have been the heat. I was hallucinating. My grumbling stomach was finally starting to affect my brain. Or perhaps I'd misprogrammed the communication nanites after all.

The voices sounded again.

I looked at the interface. I had nearly all the suspiciously Resurgence-related files from the University fileshare. I'd thought about email, but that probably *would* tip someone off.

I minimized the holograms and latched the computer to my hip. Very carefully, I crept toward the vertex of the triangle wall.

The voices grew louder. I dared a peek around the corner.

Taro and another guy sat against the wall, each red and sweaty, wearing nothing. Their clothes lay in a pile beside them.

I turned away. Shit, shit, shit. Of all the people...

"Can you believe they're going to choose another Messenger this year?" the one I didn't recognize asked.

"Yeah," Taro said.

"What do you think the Resurgence will do?"

"Dunno."

"I want to rise up the ranks one day. We'll show those idiot zealots."

"Yup."

I rolled my eyes. *Try not to sound so excited, you emotional black hole.*

"I heard the higher ups are planning something big," the other guy said. "Really big."

"Yeah?"

"Maybe I won't need to show the Monastery guys after all. Maybe someone's going to get rid of them for good."

"Who told you that?"

The great Taro had awoken! I squirmed, giddy that

someone, at least, had managed to rouse a response from him.

"A friend."

"Tell me."

I couldn't see either of them, and neither of them spoke. I dared another look. The two of them were making out. I turned away, feeling dirtier than ever. I felt even grosser than ever for having been with Taro for so long.

I glance at my computer screen. All downloaded.

I crept away, as silently as I could and tried to focus on coming up with a comfortable place where I could study nanite programming. My thoughts kept drifting back to what Taro's new friend had said.

What if he were right?

I ran down the crimson halls at the top safe speed, though it was a struggle not to push myself harder. I had once tried top speed in the hallways and had collided with a scientist. She hadn't been happy.

"Hey Stok!" one of the lab staff smiled. His voice was barely more than a passing blur. "Congrats, man!"

I smiled and ran faster. I hurtled into the infirmary and rushed up to Kish's side. She held Mox in her arms, swaddled in linens. I beamed proudly. Sadness mixed in. I'd missed him being born. I couldn't believe I'd missed it.

"I'm... sorry, Kish."

She shot me a bemused look. "And if you had stayed here, we'd all have been eaten alive by evolvers now, wouldn't we?"

"Uh, yeah, I guess."

"Life on Asura." She looked into Mox's eyes, then looked up at me. "You want to hold him?"

I beamed. I took him up in my arms. He smiled and giggled. I held out my finger, bulbous and silvery as it may be, and he clutched it. He looked up into my face, and he smiled.

He was amazing. I hadn't felt this human in forever.

I handed him back to Kish in a daze. I'd never imagined my life with a child until nine months ago. Now I couldn't imagine my life without Mox. And I'd only just met him.

Thoughts of my imminent departure swirled in my head. The odds were all over the place. The computerminds gave the deranged a good chance of evolving us all, regardless of team size. The location of the portal was simply too exposed. There would be no cover, just a wide open plain with a few hills.

"When are you leaving?" Kish asked.

"In a few hours."

She frowned. Conflicting emotions tore across her face.

"The computerminds say the sooner we go the better. We've got 0.03 percent odds improvement if we leave before sunset."

She shook her head. "Any advantage you can get, huh?"

"It's all I've got."

"Come back for him."

"I will."

Mox reached out his tiny little hands toward me and burbled happily. I lost myself in his beautiful, innocent eyes. I'd make these next two hours ones to remember.

Hey Le?

Yeah, I'm here.

Awesome. How you holding up?

Pretty well. The food is shit, but I suppose it's better than starving.

You're telling me. My stomach has been hurting all day. I haven't had a decent meal since... Logic, I don't remember. Was it three days ago?

Focus on getting yourself food, Shey. Are you at least getting water?

Yeah. I've been down to the shelter a few times. Saw my dad there this morning, though, and had to duck out the fire escape. Haven't been back since.

You need to eat.

I will. I'm... uh... calling because—

Calling? Is that what this is?

Le!

Yeah?

I'm about to open the file with the details for their plan.

Cool. Probably some policy reform or something, right? They're going to make Messengers illegal, maybe cancel

Monastery holidays?

I heard something earlier. Something more ominous. I hope you're right. Regardless of what it is, I'm still trying to break you out, okay?

Yeah.

Really!

How about you open the document?

...

Shey?

Yeah?

Well, what's in the document?

It's a list of chemicals...

What kind of chemicals?

... Logic save us...

Shey...?

They're going to implode the portal.

What?!

They want to send the entire Monastery hill to Asura and close the portal for good.

The blue dot representing me on my overlay aligned with the blue cross marking the location of the portal. The wind whipped across the landscape of hills and metallic grass. It seemed oddly familiar, even though I knew the terraforming evolvers must have reshaped the topography dozens if not hundreds of times over the last twelve months.

The other six soldiers of my contingent took up positions around me.

"I don't see anything," one shouted.

"Be happy it stays that way," another shouted.

Indeed, my overlay was remarkably free of green dots.

I got to work, the sound of ammunition clusters being unpacked all around me. The six others stood around me in a circle at even intervals. I tried not to think about what they were doing for me. They knew. Oh, how they must have known.

I applied the first layer of resonance frequencies to the distortion. No effect. I began running others. I set up a queue to go through them in sequence, then try random combinations. It'd take at least five minutes to go through them all.

"Incoming!" One of the soldiers cried out.

Gunfire erupted.

Green dots on my overlay. I tried to ignore them.

I looked at the hillside before me. The portal should have been just a few meters in front of my face, a little above the ground. I saw only empty space, the cold, dead earth and silver grass.

The gunfire grew more intense, mixed with the shrill cry of the deranged.

"C'mon," I grumbled. Finding nothing left to do with the computer, I picked up my rifle and began taking pot shots at the deranged. They'd completely encircled us. What these soldiers must be feeling right now.

I knew what drove me on—Mox and grandpa and Le and Kish and Tarangar. I'd go to the end of the universe for any one of them.

Blue light crackled beside me momentarily, and then it was gone.

I threw down my rifle and returned to the computer.

"Stok, we could really use the help," a soldier shouted.

"Just a second," I shouted back.

The blue flash had occurred during a pair of two particular resonance frequencies. I modified my program to move all combinations containing those frequencies to the front of the queue.

I picked up my rifle and fired again. Two, four, eight, sixteen down, and they just kept coming.

"I'm down!" a soldier screamed, her voice turning metallic mid-sentence.

She caught a bolt in the chest from a fellow soldier, just as a deranged hauled him up into the air. His body glittered against the crimson sky, elongating and turning silver.

"*Inferus becomes superus!*" the creature shrieked.

I shot it. And I shot my former friend, too.

More screams as my friends turned to enemies all around me. The deranged surged toward me.

Blue light erupted from beside me.

I looked into it, a glowing sphere, just the same as it the one I'd walked into in the Monastery so many months ago.

I glanced about. No one moved. Not even the deranged.

I shifted my weight and lunged for the portal.

Something grabbed me by the leg, and I crashed into the ground. Inside my head, I shrieked in blind rage. *Don't let me die here! Don't let me my son grow up without a father! Let me see Le again! Divine One, let me see Le and our beautiful desert again, please!*

My hand found my rifle. I picked it up and shot wildly in all directions. Deranged shrieks pierced the air.

I stood and leapt again.

The maroon sky and brown hills flashed away, and I found myself encased in swirling blue.

I looked down at my feet, and I wept tears anew. Silver veins traced their way up my leg. They reached my stomach, and my insides contorted. I cried out in pain. Metallic spikes tore out of my skin, blossoming from my chest, and in that moment both sight and consciousness flickered out to nothing.

FAITH

[Le]

I can't remember not being busy. Not ever.

In primary and secondary school, I was constantly working with computers, writing programs, playing void-ball, going on camping trips, hanging out with friends. Always something to do.

Then I'd met Stok, and he'd become the center of my life for two glorious weeks.

And then Monastery, with its strict regimen, taught me the value of routine, the value of normalization and standardization, a purity and clarity of thought that had been extremely welcome in Stok's absence.

And now, a small, white, plastic room with no windows and one door. It was amazingly quiet.

A little too quiet, after a time. Just when solitude and contemplation had started to drift toward madness, Shey's voice had burst into my mind. Oh, Shey. At the very least, you've got a friend for life.

I stared up at the blank white ceiling, reflecting on my

previous lives. To be nineteen years old and already have previous lives... I shook my head.

I thought back to Stok. I wondered if that's how he felt about his time with me here. Was it now a distant memory, some previous life? Did he yearn to come back, like he'd promised, or had he found new love, new adventure in the wild unknown of Asura, the land that Writ promised to be a veritable paradise, the harmonious coexistence of humans of all ideologies?

Or so it was written. If that were the case, why hadn't anyone returned to tell us about it and take us home? Or at the very least establish some kind of relationship? Had our ancestors really been *that* bad?

So many questions, and just one, blank, white ceiling.

The ceiling never provided answers. It just was.

Sounds emanated from beyond the door, like heavy logs falling to the ground.

I ran to the door and peered out its tiny window. Four guards lay slumped on the linoleum floor, their eyes closed.

Shey stood among them. He smiled up at me.

"Shey!" I smiled back. "Open the door!"

"What?" His voice was extremely muted.

I rolled my eyes at him.

He searched the guards, removed a keycard from one and ran to the door panel. I backed up, and the door swung open.

I hugged him. "Thank you."

"You bet."

"How'd you do that?"

He pumped his eyebrows. "I wrote my own nanite program."

I shook my head, eyes wide. "Shey... no."

"Everyone who gets within five meters of me, except for you, falls instantly asleep."

I widened my eyes. "Divine One save us, Shey. What if you put one of them into a coma?"

"It's just putting a common soporific into their bloodstream! Nothing to worry about."

"There should be rules for how people use these things... don't you think?"

Shey sighed. "Sure, but let's worry about *after* we stop the Resurgence."

I sighed. "Sure. Okay. Let's go."

"Freeze!" A voice from the hallway's far door.

"Logic, not again," Shey said.

"Hands in the air!" the policeman said.

I raised my hands. So did Shey.

The policeman edged toward us, gun pointed at us.

"Stay right where you are," he said.

Shey sighed.

They're moving slower each time, I heard Shey think.

After an excruciatingly tedious wait, the policeman edged within Shey's five meter radius and fell face-first to the floor.

"C'mon," Shey said. "Let's get out of here."

I followed him out of the hall and into the station lobby.

Everywhere, I spotted people asleep in their chairs, slumped against walls. The police station wouldn't be handling emergencies anytime soon. I wondered how we might get help should the portal bomb prove difficult to disarm.

We walked through the dozing horde of bodies and directly out the front door of the police station. The sun was high in the sky. I hadn't felt the sun in three days. Its warmth felt good on my skin. I took a deep breath, expelling stale air.

"Where is everyone?" I asked. The streets lay deserted. Shops were closed.

"Today's the Festival," Shey said. He led me down the street toward the University at a quick jog.

Of course.

"So, what's our plan?" I asked.

"Break into the Monastery and nix the implosion device."

"Any idea how to do that?"

"I've got a program for that too. Check it out." He slowed to a walk, pulled his computer out of his backpack and handed it to me.

I read over the interface. "Nice. A nanite program that introduces a chemical into the mix that stifles the reaction."

"Thanks."

"Your encapsulation sucks, though. What if someone wants to modify this program later?"

Shey punched me in the shoulder. "Smart ass,"

I handed him his computer, and he returned it to his backpack, just as we rounded the University and approached the Festival.

I grabbed Shey's arm. "There are kids here, Shey. You've gotta turn off that program until we get closer to the Monastery."

"Fine, fine." He did as I asked and we continued running along the edge of the Festival, its participants happily oblivious to the impending peril. This year's class played at the various games, just like I had a year ago. Maroon and yellow-orange streamers flitted in the breeze. Still so weird to think of that time as only twelve months prior.

I found my feet slowing as we passed the track event, and my eyes clung to the runners. I found I couldn't look away, couldn't help but watch them happily running. Water welled up in my eyes.

"Le!" Shey grabbed my arm.

"Sorry." I sniffled, wiped my eyes, and continued alongside him.

When we reached the Monastery hill, Shey turned his program back on. We walked up to the Monastery guards, and they collapsed. The same with reception. I hoped Master Nurla was down at the Festival.

I took the lead, and Shey hurried down the halls after me. Finally, we came to the door with the dozen locks that glowed blue at its edges. There were eight monk guards, tall, burly men, all of whom toppled at our approach.

"So, what now?" I asked. I can't open those locks.

"Just like before," Shey said. "Search the guards."

I crouched over one of the monks and searched his pockets. Nothing.

"Le!" Master Nurla's voice called out.

Damn it, I thought. *I really wish you were down at the Festival.*

She stood at the end of the hall, the dim blue light casting shadows over her fearful features. "Initiate Le, what are you doing?"

"We need into the portal room. The Resurgence planted an implosion device. They want to send the whole Monastery to Asura."

"That's absurd!" She marched forward.

"Don't come any closer!" I yelled, and she stopped.

"Why?"

"It's dangerous."

"Initiate Le, there is no implosion device—"

"Then prove me wrong!" I turned to Shey. "Turn off the program."

He screwed up his face. "What?"

"Turn it off! Trust me."

He huffed and pulled out his computer.

"Master Nurla," I said. "You've taught me so much. I've done my best to be a good initiate for you, and I know I don't have the best aptitude for literature and history, but I do have an aptitude for computers, and I know that something very bad will happen to the portal if we don't open this door and disarm that device."

Nurla strode right up to me, mere inches from my body. She nodded to Shey. "He's from the University. You've been duped. He wants access to the portal—!"

"No!" I threw up my hands.

"I wouldn't do that," Shey said meekly. "I want to save lives. I—I don't want to end up like my father!"

Nurla's eyes danced between both our pleading expressions. Her shoulders fell. She sighed, turned and approached the door. She pulled a monktech cube from her pocket, placed it on her right palm and held it aloft. Each of the locks clicked open in turn.

She stepped back and the door swung open.

A blue sphere wobbled in the air, a small flight of stone steps leading up to it.

"See? There is no— Divine One in Nirvana!" She tapped out commands on her cube, and a siren erupted, the one we'd used for evacuation drills.

Shey ran up to a small, black box that sat at the base of the steps with blinking lights. Shey pulled out his computer and began typing. I joined him.

"You can disarm that thing?" Nurla asked.

I turned to her. "Yes."

"How?" She wore a befuddled expression.

"We have its specs," I said.

I helped Shey with the code. We triple checked everything, testing and retesting even the most innocuous algorithms. We had to get this absolutely right or people would die. How some people think programming is boring I have no idea.

I nodded to Shey, and his finger stabbed the 'execute' button on his computer. Our eyes shot to the box on the stairs. Its lights blinked, and blinked, and blinked... and then stopped.

Shey and I expelled sighs.

I held up my hand for a high five, and his hand met mine.

We walked down the steps triumphantly.

Nurla eyed us warily. "First, how did you even know—"

The oscillation of the blue glow from the portal increased in speed. It glowed brighter.

Master Nurla and I fell to our knees and held our hands before us. We chanted in unison. "Divine One in Nirvana, we are honored to accept your humble servant from the alternate universe Asura, our former home, the place of all righteousness, your divine temple."

"*Divine One* save us..." Shey looked between us and the blue orb, baffled. Blue flashes cast his astounded features in an intermittent strobe effect. "Someone's coming through? I couldn't have done that, could I?"

I stood up. Master Nurla continued to pray.

"I don't see how."

The portal surged, and a body fell out, huge and metallic. Its legs, arms, and chest were engorged, its head and arms elongated, and its hands were twisted claws. Metallic spikes protruded from its chest.

Shey twisted up his face. "What the—?"

The creature screeched a harsh, metallic scream, and veins of metal surged off it, encompassing the stairs, the walls, everything.

"Master Nurla!" I pulled her to her feet and pointed to the lines of silver, stretching out across the ground. "Run!"

She, Shey and I took off away from the scene. The creature screeched again, and then so did the guards who'd fallen asleep.

We ran toward the entrance, occasionally looking back, only to find the veins of silver trailing in our wake. The metallic shrill cry of the creature continued, only growing more distant as we ran.

"What *was* that thing?" Master Nurla asked.

"No idea!" Shey and I said in unison.

"All we did was deactivate the device," Shey said. "That was it."

At the entrance to the Monastery I picked up the unconscious receptionist and slung her over my shoulder. Shey and Nurla took one of the monk guards.

We hauled them out onto the sand, then turned and watched. All of us wondered the same thing, I'm sure: would the metal veins proceed beyond the Monastery? Would they eat up the entire city? The whole of River Province?

The veins traced their way up the sides of the Monastery, eating away centuries-old carvings and statues, morphing it all into a metallic cacophony of spikes and cylinders and meshes.

The veins indeed stayed within the confines of the building. The people left inside morphed and twisted too, converted to metal along with everything else.

"W-What do we do now?" Shey asked.

Master Nurla bit her lip and shook her head, and we all looked up at our former Monastery.

The Festival was halted. The police were roused from slumber, and every available officer converged on the Monastery. Shey, Master Nurla, and I were held at the scene. They asked us the same questions over and over. We told the story of what happened endlessly.

At some point, a man in a fancy plastic suit with an air tank on his back showed up.

He stepped over the threshold into the Monastery in his protective outfit, and the metal veined up his legs. He was gone in a matter of seconds.

My third time through the story of what happened, I looked up at the Monastery walls. If I hadn't known better, I'd have thought I'd seen metallic lips. They moved up and down, then disappeared in a nanotech haze.

The sun grew low in the sky. No one knew what to do. The metal remained in and on the Monastery, but no one felt safe. Half the police contingent disappeared. They talked about evacuating Rig except for emergency person-nel, or urging Parliament to order emergency construction of zone walls for the Monastery.

I sat and watched the ever-shifting metallic horror.

"Hey." Shey put a hand on my shoulder.

"Hi." I shivered, even though it wasn't cold.

"How you holding up?" he asked.

"Best as can be expected."

He nodded.

I spotted something and pointed. "You see that?"

"Yeah! You noticed that too? I thought I saw an eye earlier. And an ear, too."

"And lips?"

"Yeah, lips. And they moved."

I nudged him with my arm. He looked at me and I tapped at the side of my head.

He fiddled with his computer.

Yeah?

If the nanites can make sounds, like in our eardrums, can they record them?

Yeah. I think I saw that in with the other nanite programs.

Can you get one of our nanites close enough to those lips to see if they're saying something?

Shey smiled. *Yeah, I think so. C'mon, help me.*

We sat as the light waned, the little holographic interface before us, and we coded. The recording of sound we had. The pattern matcher that would find the lips when they appeared was harder, but brought fond memories of computer science homework with Shey.

After sunset, we finally had it. We set the program to

work, and waited with bated breath.

A policeman appeared behind us. "You two can go home now. I don't think we're going to accomplish anything else here tonight, and you'd be safer if you got on one of the buses to Yajur or Sama."

"Thank you," I said. "Just a few more minutes, then we'll go."

"Okay," he said. "But at the first sign of trouble, I'm hauling you out myself."

We turned back to Shey's computer interface.

He smiled. "Got one."

Muffled noise emanated from the computer speakers.

"Turn up the volume," I suggested.

He played it again. Still unintelligible.

"Didn't we do audio filtering in eleventh year?" I asked.

Shey snapped his fingers. "I still have those programs. Just a sec."

He played the file again. Almost sounded like a word now, a single syllable.

"One more pass," Shey said.

He played it again.

"*Le!*" the computer recording said.

I clasped my hand over my mouth. My eyes welled up with tears.

"Oh... Oh my... Divine One... *That's Stok?*"

Shey put his arm around me, but I fell to the ground sobbing. Shey knelt beside me. "Le..."

I stood up. I gazed over the writhing, gray structure that had been my home for the last year.

I walked toward the entrance. Shey walked beside me.

"Hey!" voices shouted. Police ran up to me, standing between me and the entrance to the Monastery, just five meters away.

"Initiate Le," the policeman said. "I can't let you do this."

"You will." I took a step forward.

He clutched my shoulder, stopping me. "I won't let you kill yourself."

I pointed to the Monastery. "That's Stok."

The policeman blinked at me. "That— *That's* Messenger Stok?"

I nodded. "He's calling my name, and I love him. So, you can either arrest me, or you can let me go inside."

The policeman looked to other members of authority around him. He removed his hand from my shoulder and stepped aside, a look of extreme unease plastered across his face.

Shey grabbed my hand. "You sure you want to do this?"

I nodded.

He hugged me. "Good luck in there."

"Thank you, Shey." I hugged him back.

I stepped up to the Monastery threshold. Just centimeters away, the ground crawled with metallic veins.

Feel, but don't feel. Think, but don't think. Then act. I

remember, Stok. I remember.

I took a deep breath, stepped forward, and brought my foot down. I stood atop the seething metallic floor.

I looked down. My feet remained my own.

A few more breaths to calm myself, and I strode into the Monastery. The hallways were pitch black, as all the lighting had been absorbed, but I managed most of the corners from memory. Once I misjudged a turn and ran smack into a wall, but no matter what I touched, my body remained my own.

As I approached the portal, the blue glow illuminated the corridors, and I picked up my pace. The metallic man lay in a heap before the stair and the enormous, open door.

I ran to him.

"Stok?" I asked.

The creature looked up at me with empty orange eyes, and it stared. I didn't recognize the face or the arms. They were long and veiny, with huge claws for hands and feet. The eyes were narrow slits. If there was some emotion behind them, I couldn't discern it.

It stared at me.

"Is that you, Stok?" Tears brimmed my eyes.

Its gaze remained blank.

"Damn it!" I sobbed. "Say something!"

It grabbed my arm, and the metallic veins crawled up my crimson robes, spreading to my hand, my shoulder, my chest, my head. I jerked away, screamed, lost my sight, and shrieked, howling until my voice turned metallic.

My voice ebbed, and consciousness slipped away.

"Le?" Stok's voice. "Le?"

I lurched upright. I stood on white. Everything was white. White all around. Computer code hung in the air, giant red letters, some characters and symbols were the size of my head, others tiny, barely discernible, and every size in between. The code floated about the space.

"Le?" from behind me.

"*Stok!*"

I turned and saw him. He wore his wickshirt and his shorts, had the same dark hair and kind eyes. I ran to him, and we grabbed each other up in one another's arms. We sobbed into one another's shirts. I held him so tightly.

"I'm so sorry, Le. I shouldn't have left."

"Don't worry, Stok. I'm just so glad to see you again."

"Really though," Stok sniffled and held me arm's length. "Not yet. We can't do this yet. So many people still in trouble, Le."

"What do you mean?" I asked.

"Asura..." Stok shook his head. "It's not a paradise at all."

"Tell me about it."

"When there's more time. Right now, there's something I need you to do."

"What's that?"

"Get the zone walls. Bring them to the portal and chuck them through. I couldn't control what happened before with the people in the Monastery when I arrived and the man who entered... and I'm sorry about that. This stuff..." He gestured to the computer code and bunched up his features like he might cry again. "...I think it's replacing my consciousness, and I'm thinking in it, so I can change it, but I don't really know how it works. I only barely figured out where the Monastery boundaries were and kept everything inside."

I grabbed his shoulders. "I'll tell you what all this does! We can fix it together. I mean, if we get rid of the code, that metal around the monastery will go away, and you'll go back to normal, right?"

Stok shook his head. "We can't do that either. Not yet. I'm not just keeping the evolvers inside the Monastery, I'm keeping the deranged from coming through the portal on Asura. If I lose the connection to the portal, I can't keep them out—"

"Evolvers? Deranged?"

"Long story. They're terrible, Le. You have no idea how bad. We need to send the zone walls through and set them up around the portal on the Asura side. Then you can help me with all this." He gestured to the floating red letters.

I traced his logic in the air with my fingers. "Because the zone walls will keep these deranged things from getting into the portal?"

Stok nodded happily.

I frowned and threw up my hands. "How am I sup-

206

posed to convince them to dismantle the walls? They can't even agree to disagree!"

"You'll have to make them," Stok said, then frowned. "This code is winning against me, Le. And at that point, the evolvers will overrun Rig, River Province, and the entire planet, and you and everyone else will get turned into deranged."

I grinned through tears and winked at him. "Okay. I'll find a way."

He grinned back and embraced me again. He felt so good. I'd dreamed of this moment for twelve months, just never quite like this.

"Le?"

"Yeah?"

"I have so much to tell you about. Is there... do you want me to come back to Alterra and be in your life?"

"Yes, Stok." I cried tears of joy. "Yes, I do."

I walked out of the Monastery into a night awash with the blue-red glare of police car lights and the piercing beams of headlights. Momentarily, I realized it was not just police cars but also military vehicles that hard surrounded the Monastery entrance. I stepped off the Monastery entrance and onto the crunching sand to audible gasps and murmurs.

Shey ran up to me and hugged me.

"Did you see him?" he whispered in my ear.

I nodded. I turned to the policeman. "I need to call an

emergency session of Parliament. Now."

The police men and women looked between one another. I wasn't sure if they were in shock or about to laugh in my face.

The one I'd spoken to earlier opened the door to his jeep, and pulled out a handy.

He tapped on its interface. "Hi. Yes. Get the chief. Tell him that the kid who went into the Monastery just walked out, and he wants an emergency session of Parliament. ... Yes. Yes, I know what's happened. Let me repeat that for you. The young man who was just *inside the Monastery for fifteen minutes and has walked out unscathed* wants an emergency session of Parliament."

He nodded to me, and he smiled. Shey squeezed my shoulder.

Parliament's main chamber was a great semi-circle with the representatives from the House of Analytics sitting on the left, and those from the House of Souls on the right. About two-thirds of them had already fled for Yajur or Sama, but the ones who remained had heeded my call.

I spotted Shey's father among them. He and many of the other House of Analytics reps glared up at me and my crimson robes. I pulled at Shey, and he stepped forward, standing beside me.

I took a deep breath, and I spoke into the microphone.

"My name is Le Namgyal. I come before you tonight representing neither the Monastery nor the University. I represent Alterra. I spoke with Messenger Stok Thiksay, who has returned from Asura to bring us incredible news. Far from a benevolent paradise of high culture and technology, something has happened there that has turned most humans into malevolent, heartless monstrosities called deranged whose goal is to reshape humanity in their image. They will come through the portal and attack us if Messenger Stok is not assisted in fortifying it."

I took a deep breath. "Specifically, Messenger Stok has asked that we tear down as many of the zone walls as we can and send them through the portal, myself included, where I will arrange them around the portal on their side, thus protecting it, and us, from the deranged."

Muttering turned into shouts over the center aisle.

"And give the House of Souls control over the nanites? Never! They'll set up idiotic shrines for worshipping their imaginary deities and seal the technology away from us forever!"

"The House of Analytics will use the nanites to their political advantage, and our society will plunge into further disgrace and abasement! They don't need any help from Asura. They're already 'deranged' themselves, and with similar goals!"

"Stop!" I yelled into the microphone. *"Just stop it! All of you!"* I huffed and I panted. "Enough with this *idiotic, petty* bickering about which side's ideology is right. Both of you are right! Both of you!"

I took a breath, collecting my thoughts and rallying my

passions in their aid.

"I started my education preparing for University. Teachers noticed my skills in math and computers, and encouraged me to develop those skills. I'm immensely grateful. These are the very tools we've used to build a functional, technologically advanced, thriving society in a vast desert with the meager resources of a single river valley.

"But that wasn't enough. I knew I was missing something important. Messenger Stok gave me a glimpse of it, and later Master Nurla at the Monastery immersed me in it. Religion isn't just a bunch of old superstitions—it's about art and music and imagination and cultural heritage. It's about deep, meditative thought about our existence as a species. Most practically, it's about how to be good and decent people to one another. How to avoid the perils of hubris and self-aggrandizement."

I caught a glimpse of Shey and his father glaring at one another.

"Alterra is in danger, and so is..." I paused to collect my emotions. "So is the guy I love." I clamped my teeth down hard and took a deep breath. "Please just help me do this. None of the nanites in any of the zones except D are harmful. I can attest to that. And they can be controlled with programming that any technologically savvy person can learn."

Shey grabbed the microphone. "*I* can attest to that."

"Please," I said. "Put petty politics aside for five minutes. Or however long it takes to save our planet."

I sat down and Shey took my place at the podium. "I'd like to propose a resolution, number forty-five of the tenth month of the four hundred twelfth year of Alterra. The proposal is a simple one. Eight wall segments from Zone H will be immediately transported to the portal and sent to Asura along with Initiate Le Namgyal."

Shey grinned triumphantly at his father. I turned to face Shey, and his smile turned friendly.

He nodded his congratulations to me, and Parliament voted.

So much blue all around me.

I'd never imagined I'd see the inside of the portal. I felt giddy. The movement of my vision didn't match the sensation of my head turning. And what was I standing on? What propelled me through this bizarre ocean? I tried to conjure up a mental image of endless expanses of water, like our river but stretching out toward the horizon.

This, I imagined, was probably better than that could ever be.

The blue shifted and swirled. It congealed into brown hills and maroon sky. I fell onto one of the slabs of zone wall. The slabs lay scattered, a couple here, a couple there. I turned left and right, and I counted. Eight segments. Good.

A shrill metallic shriek sounded from somewhere on my right. I turned. Three creatures crested a hill. They were many meters tall, all silver and lanky with distorted, long faces and rows of razor teeth. Their skin shimmered, fuzzy, lacking a discernible boundary, and their eyes glowed bright orange. They rushed toward me at impossible speeds, nearing me before I'd barely shuffled back.

All at once, as they came within five meters of where I lay, the three of them shrieked again, louder this time, and painfully. Something happened to their bodies that was difficult to describe. It was almost as if some force was pressing their own bodies back into themselves.

They lumbered back and fell over each other. Their bodies normalized as they retreated.

Four more creatures crested another hill and shrieked. They rushed toward me, but experienced the same effect. Their compatriots shrieked at them, and they too pulled away from me and the wall slabs.

"*Inferus!*" one said, and I turned to face it. "*What have you done, inferus?*"

I looked at the ground. At my feet and around the walls slabs, the ground was brown and dusty. Three or four meters beyond the slabs, tufts of metallic grass dotted the landscape.

Metallic things were being repelled—things made of nanites!

"Your... bodies are all nanites?" I twisted up my face.

"*We have evolved.*"

"*We are homo sapiens superus. You are homo sapiens inferus.*"

"*You are faulty.*"

"*Broken.*"

"*Without intellect or rational thought.*"

"*A barbaric stage of human development.*"

"*We will evolve you, and you will join us in brother-hood.*"

"*You will join our perfect society.*"

"Okay..." I bit my lip. "Come get me then."

More deranged crested the hills, dozens of them. The ones near me shrieked a warning to them, and they remained still.

I smiled and moved to a zone wall slab.

One of the creatures rushed toward me, came to the edge of my field of safety, its features twisted up in pain, contorting and compressing ever so slightly. But it proceeded no closer to the slab of metal that lay between us.

"*Stop,*" it said. "*Do not do this. Let us through.*"

I stood tall, my eyes locked with its. I can't remember ever having been more afraid than just then. My heart must have been beating miles a minute. But then I gazed over the creature before me. If I didn't know better, I'd have guessed from its elongated metallic face that it was afraid. Even the holograms that darted across its hazy, gray skin seemed fervent and jittery.

"Stok's in trouble. Why should I?"

"*You will never know beauty. Or truth. We understand our world, our universe, deeper than the subatomic, deeper than the quantum. We can show you. We can show all your kind immeasurable beauty and grandeur. We can give you unparalleled comprehension of the cosmos. If only you will let us. We can free you from your self-imposed oppression."*

I gulped and bit my lip. "Can you show me without changing my body? Can you change my mind with logic and reasoning, or do you have to destroy me to get me to agree with you?"

"Your form is inferior! You must be evolved. There is no other way."

I frowned and took a step forward. I wrapped my hands under the gritty edges of the metal wall slab and hauled it to a stance.

The deranged shrieked, but drew no closer while I erected the remaining slabs in a circle around the portal.

I opened my eyes.

Stok sat on his knees in the white space, his hands wrapped around his head.

Red code surged all around him, symbols everywhere, a veritable ocean of them, much thicker than before.

I ran to him, pushing letters, numbers and punctuation out of my way.

I grabbed his hands and pulled him up.

"Stok..."

"Hi, Le." His voice trembled.

"Stok, you can stop now. I set up the walls, and I sent the message to your friends. A guy named Nohar said he'd bring reinforcements. The Asura portal is safe. And those things outside the walls... Divine One save us, you *lived* there for a year?"

Stok nodded idly. He sobbed, his tears falling through lines of red code. "I'm sorry, Le. I-I'm not sure what's left of me. We could tear this all apart... but what if it's already replaced my mind? What if there's no 'me' left?"

He grabbed my hands and looked into my eyes. "After this, you have to take more walls to Asura. You have to. Promise me. For my son."

My eyes widened. "Your son?!" Shock struck me. My mouth hung agape.

Stok slunk away from me, rubbed his shoulders, stared at the floor and bit his lip.

I grabbed him up in my arms again. "Stok, look at me. Look at me!"

He did.

I smiled at him. "I love you, Stok. I meant what I said about wanting to be with you. About your son..." I took a deep breath. "You've got to tell me all about him. After we fix you up. See this line?" I pointed at a large chunk of code encased in curly braces. "I recognize that from working with Shey—"

"You and Shey made up?"

"We're friends. Another long story."

He looked away, and I squeezed his shoulders tighter. "You're going to hear about it when we're done."

He nodded weakly. His eyes turned dark and serious. "I can show you the code. All of it."

"Okay."

"It'll probably be intense."

"I've come this far, haven't I?"

He reached out tentatively, feared etched into his features, and he touched his hand to my head. My vision went black. It felt as though all of the red letters and numbers and symbols were rushing into my brain all at once. A massive amount of data, thousands of lines, all one big jumble.

I seized up. My heart skipped a beat. I gasped.

Gradually, the cluster unraveled. I pulled at its edges and began to recognize forms—objects and functions. I spotted a segment of code I recognized, then another. I pulled one block to the fore, using only my mental will. This one wasn't for humans at all. Where did it link in? Ah, okay. Move that segment, change that reference. Good. Deleted. Gone. One down. A couple thousand more to go.

"Le?"

"Yeah, Stok?"

"You know what you're doing, right?"

"Yup."

"My life's in your hands, Le."

"I won't let anything happen to you, Stok."

"Le... Thank you."

I sat on the floor of the Monastery with a metallic man. The metal lines receded all around us, leaving stone and fresco and flourish in their wake.

The metallic spikes in the man's chest melted and his stature diminished, but he remained a head taller than me. His hands and feet shrank too, though not completely to human proportions. His fingers were too big and still covered in metal. His chest was massive, his shoulders wide. His face normalized, the metal tracing away, and his legs returned to their right proportions, though they too were large and also covered with metal. He had claws for hands and feet.

I smiled up at his familiar face. "Stok?"

He gulped and looked down at me. "This is... I'm like this now." He had his same sweet voice, just like before. I hugged him, the metallic part of his chest was cold, but I didn't care. I wept, and so did he.

"I'm sorry about this... I had to... I mean, for the people I care about on Asura."

"I don't care what you look like," I said. "I'm so happy you're safe."

He held me in his massive arms. "I still have a lot of work to do. I know it's a lot to ask, since I didn't give you your journey up the river, but will you come with me, back and forth between Asura and here? Help them build more walls? Meet my son?"

I nodded. "Yeah. Yeah, I'd like that."

I took his hand, bulky and huge, and we walked to the Monastery entrance. He held his free hand up against the morning sun.

"I forgot how bright it was." He squinted, and I smiled

wide.

The policeman and monks gawked at Stok, and I squeezed his hand. More police cars pulled up, the sleek black cars of Parliament reps, too. Military personnel and politicians exited their vehicles and walked up to us, staring at Stok and mumbling to one another.

"My fellow Alterrans," I announced. "Messenger Stok Thiksay has come home."

EPILOGUE

Stok and I took the lead transporting the rest of Alterra's zone wall slabs to Asura, all except Zone D's. Shey was re-admitted to the University and started a study group for nanite code. Once Shey and his group had incapacitated the chlorine producing nanites, Stok and I took over transporting those wall segments as well.

While many Alterran groups took an interest in the zone land for commercialization, an intense debate ensued in Parliament. Stok and I fought for retaining Zones A, F, H and J as parks, and we won. Zone H held a special interest for us both, naturally. We made sure the floating nanite lights that sparked when they collided remained a permanent fixture, and gave the hilly overlook benches, a fence, and flowers.

Shey's study group at the University eventually became the Alterran Nanoprogramming Research and Ethics Council, and at my behest, he included members from the Monastery as well. Even if unskilled at programming, those members were tasked with sitting in on activities meetings and feature development, to give voice to any moral or ethical concerns that might arise.

Shey led the group with vigor, albeit a bit of pomp, which he admitted to inheriting from his father. Those two never saw completely eye to eye, but they did begin speaking to each other again after full diplomatic relations with Asura were established.

Stok, Shey and I travelled between Alterra and Asura frequently. Shey took a keen interest in the men with the nanogenic enhancements to their upper bodies. He helped Nohar discover his bisexuality, but that lasted only a short time, and Nohar eventually fell for an Alterran woman.

One day, a man named Rayad showed up at the periphery of A5. He hailed from the distant outpost E1 and had heard of the shield walls in passing. He marveled at our outpost's fortifications, how they repelled the deranged and the evolvers both, and how no one had to sacrifice their consciousness to do it.

Shey took to Rayad immediately. He even acquired the nanogenic leg enhancements so he could make the trip with Rayad back to his home outpost, where the two of them helped emigrate those people to A5. Shey and Rayad returned from the trip married, just months after Stok and I had tied the knot.

A year after unification, Kish and Mox followed the majority of Asuran families in relocating to Alterra. Stok took over operation of A5 for only a couple of months. The outpost around the Asuran portal had become a small town. Stok and I oversaw A5's dismantlement.

The Asuran refugee parents loved Alterra's primary and secondary schools, but their children refused to choose either University or Monastery, knowing full well the folly of that perilous divide.

By the time Mox entered post-secondary education, the University and the Monastery had become one entity—the Institute. Mox excelled at history and literature, like his father, and travelled all over Asura and Alterra, the first to construct a coherent history of the two worlds.

I took a liking to Mox the moment I met him as a baby. As a small child, he loved hearing me tell stories about Dad Stok, especially the one where Dad Stok convinced Dad Le to jump off a cliff for him.

"Don't make *me* jump off a cliff, daddy!" Mox would shout.

"Don't worry," Stok said. "Our Divine One doesn't tell us to do stupid things like that anymore... most of the time." Then he'd wink and Mox would run away screaming and giggling madly.

We were there for Mox a lot as during his primary school years, but as the 'portal town' became 'Portal City,' we found ourselves with much less time on Alterra. Kish became his primary caregiver during his secondary education, but Stok and I made up for it by guiding him on a personalized tour of Asura for three years after his Institute studies.

I eventually caved and took the nanogenic leg enhancements, too, just to make travel between the various parts of Asura safe, but by the time Mox was in his twenties, the deranged no longer attacked human travelers. They huddled in enclaves somewhere, we believed, searching physics and chemistry for a way to defeat the shield walls.

Perhaps one day they would succeed, but that day never came during my lifetime.

When Stok and I reached our sixties, we undid the nanogenic enhancements and returned to our original human forms. Asura had been producing their own altered iron for two decades and had established roads between various cities lined with shield walls.

I have to admit, I was at first disconcerted when I heard the story of Mox's conception, but as I grew older I came to understand Stok and Kish's reasons. Camaraderie and friendship combined with a culture extremely concerned with procreation had led to decisions that I never faulted Stok for. And I loved Mox dearly.

What Stok never did seem to forgive himself for in all our years together was having left me to become Alterra's Messenger. He said it was the hardest decision he'd ever made, and if he had to do it over again, he wouldn't have.

I argued with him whenever he brought it up. "How can you say that? Mox wouldn't exist. The deranged could have destroyed humanity on Asura. They might have even opened the portal and come after Alterra!"

He shook his head. "I felt, I thought, I leapt. But I ignored you. I ignored love. I'm not sure I deserve all that I have."

"You do," I said. "You're a hero. I won't pretend I wasn't sad that you left, but you accomplished so much. We changed the world for the better, just like we wanted to!"

I felt. I thought. I leapt.

In the end, it brought us together just as much as it tore us apart. Within both religion and technology lay the power for destruction and creation, devastation and awe, debasement and enlightenment.

If there were third or fourth or fifth ways for me to discover, I never found them. I had Stok and Mox, my friendships with Kish, Shey and Rayad. I had a city to build. I guess if I had found a new ideology though, there would have been no need to give it a classification or a title.

From the day Stok returned, my experiences were human experiences. And that was good enough for me.